I0718357

Call:
Pied Piper Retold

DEMELZA CARLTON

A tale in the Romance a Medieval Fairy Tale series

This is a work of fiction. Names, characters, businesses, places, events and incidents are either the products of the author's imagination or used in a fictitious manner. Any resemblance to actual persons, living or dead, or actual events is purely coincidental.

Copyright © 2020 Demelza Carlton

Lost Plot Press

All rights reserved.

ISBN-13: 978-1-925799-33-0

DEDICATION

This one is for Stephanie and Rebecca
Because you asked for it.

One

"Another one full!" Sara said, carefully tipping the contents of her apron into the sack. The peeled chestnuts cascaded dutifully down onto their fellows, before Sara tied off the top of the sack so she could carry it to the cart. The chestnut harvest had been good this year, and they'd have plenty of flour to see them through 'til spring. Once these had been milled, of course.

"How do you peel them so fast?" Silvana

said, staring at her half-full basket. She stabbed her knife into a shell and the nut jumped out, surprising her.

"Practice, and knowing which ones are ready, and which need more time," Sara answered. She seized her empty basket and headed up to the smoke house. She breathed deeply as she ascended the stairs to the upper level, where the racks of sweet-smelling chestnuts dried over the smoke from their smouldering shells on the level below.

It took her right back to her childhood, when her grandfather had first brought her in here. She'd had to stretch up onto her toes to see the rows of round nuts lined up on the racks, and the one that burst open before her eyes. She'd squealed at the glimpse of creamy gold flesh amid all that brown, and her grandfather had helped her peel the nut and take it home.

If she'd known then that she'd inherit the smoke house, along with all the rest of her family's holdings, when sickness had carried away her parents and all her siblings in one horrible summer, and she'd struggled through her first autumn harvest alone, she might have been less excited about that first visit.

But grief no longer stabbed at her heart as it had all those years ago, and she'd spent every harvest since shelling nuts with Tola and Maria, Silvana's mother, until one cold winter's night, when the reaper had called for Maria, too.

If only she had a daughter who would take her place at the table with Silvana, and Tola's daughter Swanhild, when she was gone. Though the way fate had shaped her life so far, Sara herself would probably teach Silvana and Swanhild's daughters to shell the nuts, her fingers as gnarled as the chestnut kernels themselves.

Sara shook herself. Such thoughts were silly. She had no need of a daughter – she had a fine son. Tobias would be a man soon enough, ready to marry and have children of his own. If only his father had lived long enough to see him…

Were those tears on her cheeks? Surely not. It was perspiration from the heat in here. She should fill her basket quickly and head back outside.

By the time she reached the cooler air outside, Silvana had emptied her basket and was headed into the smoke house for a refill.

"Can you teach me to choose the right ones? Both you and Tola work so much faster than me. I'll never be good enough…" Silvana's eyes brimmed with tears.

Sara pried the basket from the girl's hands. "Your mother was always the slowest of the three of us when it came to peeling the nuts, but she was the best at pressing them. Here, take my basket and put them in the pressing barrel. I'll fill yours for you."

"Really?"

Sara gave a nod, and the girl hastened back to the table where Tola still sat.

The morning passed quickly, until the cart could hold no more. Silvana might have spent more time stamping on the nuts in the pressing barrel than picking or peeling them, but Sara didn't mind. She'd done her fair share of dancing in the pressing barrel when she was a girl. Now, her feet would hurt by day's end if she did Silvana's job.

"Will you join us for the midday meal?" Sara asked Silvana.

The girl shook her head, furrowing her brow. "I'll take the cart down to Father at the mill. I must make sure he has his dinner," she said.

Sara nodded. Regulo had not taken his wife's death well, and if he didn't have Silvana still, he might have followed Maria into the grave. Best the girl get home and give him some work to do.

So Sara helped Silvana harness the pony to take the cart to the mill, where Silvana and her father would turn the shelled nuts into flour, to be bagged and distributed as Sara directed. Her family might own the chestnut orchards and the smoke house, along with all the land around, but Sara made sure those who helped with the harvest received their share of the final product, to feed them through the winter. Even Silvana and her father, who took a tithe of what went through the mill. Her family had once owned the mill, too, but some wise ancestor had bequeathed the orchards to one brother and the mill to another, which made

Silvana and her father some sort of distant cousin to Sara, several times removed.

"What's in the pot?" Tola asked, bringing Sara's thoughts back to her own home.

Sara grinned. "I hope you're not sick of chestnuts. I popped some in the pot, along with the peas I shelled this morning and the last of the bacon. It should have thickened nicely by now. Perfect with some bread."

Tola's eyebrows rose. "You're out of bacon already?"

"Tobias eats enough for three men, though he's still a boy. He'll have to do without for a few weeks. As soon as we've cleared the smoke house, Cronus will slaughter some pigs for me and hang them up to smoke. They're fattening up in the forest on fallen chestnuts as we speak."

"Whereas Swanhild eats like a bird. I'd fear for her health, if she didn't spend most days in the forest, harvesting herbs. There's food aplenty for those that know how to find it, and she must." Tola shook her head, then sniffed deeply. "Oh, it is definitely time to eat."

They took their bowls outside to the table

where they'd been shelling nuts, sitting in the last of the sun before the mountain shadows stole it from them. But until it did, they enjoyed the view over the lake that lay beside the town. Today, the still surface mirrored the blue sky, illustrating perfectly why the town had earned its name of Mirroten.

"Mercurio is early," Tola remarked.

Sara sopped up the last of her stew with a crust of bread. "He's not due for weeks, and it looks too big to be his boat – are you sure?"

Tola pointed, and Sara could not deny that the ship cutting its way across the lake bore Mercurio's brightly coloured sail.

"Profits must be good, if he has bought a bigger boat."

Both women rose.

"I'd best get home and see what I have to trade. He'll have some rare ingredients from the traders in Rialto, which I've been waiting for," Tola said.

They said their farewells while Sara gathered up the dishes, but Sara lingered outside for a moment. Mercurio the merchant, sailing his boat up and down the river and through the mysterious marshes to the port of Rialto, always brought new and intriguing things from faraway lands. For a price, of course. What treasures would his ship hold this time?

A chill breeze swept down from the mountain as the sun slipped behind a cloud. Sara shivered and hurried inside.

Two

"RUN, GIRL, RUN!"

Zoticus watched the girl's expression change from panic to determined clarity. Her arms flew out like wings, letting go of everything she possessed. Before her things thudded to the ground, Melisende took flight.

He'd seen the sequence a dozen times in his visions of this moment, but somehow the addition of sound made it more real.

The scrunch of sand beneath her boots as she broke into a run, audible even over the distant screams of battle on the other side of the field. Clad in only her tunic and hose, Melisende moved so swiftly the cloth was plastered against the curves of her blatantly female body.

Eager shouts and the thunder of hooves heralded her pursuit, invisible in the crowd of panicked crusaders.

Zoticus unslung his bow and reached for his first arrow. He sighted along it, then waited.

Four riders emerged from the melee, whipping their horses hard in their frenzy for the hunt. The hunters did not know they would be the prey today.

Sir Enguerrand led the charge, a black raven atop a stolen white horse. Sir Guiscard followed some distance behind, his horse unable to keep up with the fleet-footed mare. Sir Onfroi was hot on his heels, with Sir Roland bringing up the rear on a horse that could scarcely bear his weight.

Zoticus could not abide a man who abused his mount. He lined up his shot, and Roland fell first, rolling on the ground while his relieved horse rode on without him.

Onfroi had chosen to wear armour today, so

Zoticus had to choose his target. Ah, there it was – when Onfroi leaned forward over his horse's neck, his breastplate rode up, exposing far more of his side than was safe with archers about. A kidney shot, followed by a second arrow that lodged firmly in the man's left buttock. He, too, went tumbling from the saddle, but unlike Roland, Onfroi's foot caught in the stirrup, and his horse dragged him along the ground, likely doing even more damage.

Guiscard had not bothered to don his armour, so the owl on his tunic was clear to see. Zoticus aimed for above the owl, though, and his aim was true – the first arrow caught him in the back of the neck, sinking in deep.

Enguerrand rode alone, heedless of the loss of his companions, intent only on catching the girl.

A girl whose head whipped back for scarcely a moment. Had she seen the glint of the knight's teeth, bared in a triumphant grin? Or was it her brother's horse that had made her smile before a puff of magic surrounded her, and she vanished.

Magic spirited her across the field and into

the trees, faster than any horse could gallop, but Enguerrand could not see it. Instead, he reined in his horse, casting about for the treasure he'd lost.

Only then did he realise he was alone, his men having fallen along the way.

In the space of a moment, Enguerrand seemed to regain his senses, and he fixed his sights on Zoticus. With the girl gone, he set his horse against a different target.

Zoticus stood his ground. He'd seen this in his vision, too, and he knew how it would end. He waited until he could see the horse's eyes, mad at this mistreatment from a man who was not her master.

Now.

"Halt, Pegasus!" Zoticus called, and the obedient mare skidded to a stop.

But Enguerrand did not, flying over the horse's head and over Zoticus, to land awkwardly on the stony ground.

The knight struggled to draw his sword, but he'd broken both arms in his fall. "Help me, and my father will richly reward you!" the man begged.

Zoticus leaned down and pulled Enguerrand's sword from its scabbard. It was a fine weapon – far finer than the man it had been made for. The knight would need neither sword nor scabbard now, so Zoticus unfastened the man's baldrick. More broken bones moved beneath his hand – Enguerrand had shattered several ribs, too, and at least one had punctured his lungs.

"Mercy!" cried the knight. He tried to lift his arm to shield himself, but his strength had already started to fade.

Zoticus considered the shattered man at his feet. Mercy came in many forms. A magical healer might make the knight whole again, but without swift aid he would certainly die, and die in agony.

"Did you offer Babette mercy? Or any of the other girls you hunted and killed like animals?" Zoticus asked, sliding the sword back into its scabbard before tucking both into his bag.

"Who?" the knight asked.

"Did you know any of the girls' names? No? How about Sir Josse, who you cut down with this very blade, so that you might force yourself upon his sister?" Zoticus persisted. He'd heard of men who repented their crimes when faced with death, but he had yet to meet one. Most of the men Zoticus had killed preferred to spit curses with their final breath.

It seemed Enguerrand would not be such a man, either.

"Help!" the knight moaned, trying to crawl away.

Zoticus decided to leave Enguerrand until last, and check on the others.

Guiscard stared sightlessly up at the sky, a broken arrow protruding from his throat. It had gone all the way through, as if shot from a crossbow and not a longbow. A formidable weapon indeed – no wonder the Seljuk archers were so fearsome, armed with these. Zoticus would keep his Seljuk longbow, lest it be useful later.

Onfroi's corpse was not so serene. His horse had grown weary of dragging it, and crushed the offending weight beneath his hooves. The result was that where the knight's head had once been was now a piece of pulped meat.

Roland had not been as lucky. Thrown free from his horse, his roll along the ground had torn the arrows out of his flesh, leaving gaping wounds through which his organs spilled. Much like Enguerrand, Roland's injuries were definitely mortal.

Four men dead, or they would be, by the end of the day. And every man who'd marched with them, thanks to the Seljuk army and the ambush no one but Zoticus had suspected. He could head home and collect payment for a job well done.

Ah, but he owed it to Josse to bring proof to the man's grave that his sister's violators were no more. So Zoticus collected three more swords and three signet rings, before heading back to the moaning, groaning worm that was Enguerrand.

He found Pegasus prancing around the man, shaking her head at him. It wasn't until Zoticus got closer that he realised the wretch had managed to wrap his hand around a rope trailing from the mare's bridle, and she was attempting to break free.

"Easy, Pegasus," he said, holding up his hands. He'd seen Godfrey manage this horse all the way to Byzas, and she'd seemed a biddable enough beast then. Now…

"If you'll just let me get close enough, I'll free you, and we can be on our way. I'll take you home to Godfrey and all your other stable mates," Zoticus continued.

This was apparently not to Pegasus's taste, for she reared up onto her hind legs, then brought her front hooves down hard.

Enguerrand's brains splattered on Zoticus's boots.

Pegasus tossed her head, pulling the reins from Enguerrand's slackened grasp as she stepped back from the corpse she'd created.

Zoticus pulled the ornate raven ring from Enguerrand's hand and stuffed that into his sack with everything else.

"Now, would you like me to take you home, or are you planning on joining the Seljuk army?" he asked the horse.

It was a good thing horses were not susceptible to the plague, or she never would have made it home, Zoticus thought. Nor had she liked the ship, but…

He blinked. A low wooden ceiling floated above, while straw rustled beneath him when he moved. Everything ached like Pegasus had stomped on his whole body. But he'd returned Pegasus to Godfrey long ago, before placing his sword and signet ring collection on Josse's grave.

In fact, the last time he'd felt so weak, he'd been aboard that rat-infested ship, fighting off that benighted plague that had killed off more crusaders than the Seljuks had.

Zoticus groaned. Not again. A pestilence on all plagues, for he was heartily sick of them.

Three

When Tobias left to take the goats up to the high pasture the next morning, Mercurio's stall was already under construction. Not that Mercurio himself was doing the work – oh, no, he had every labourer in town fetching and carrying for him, earning credit they might spend on his goods. Sara's brother-in-law Ahab would be among them, likely setting up the stall and directing everyone else, for it would not do for the head of the town council to be seen doing the work of a common labourer.

She shaded her eyes and peered at the hive of activity on the lake shore. Ah, good, Mercurio had brought the winter fodder for the town. They'd had a warm, dry summer up in the mountains, but you could never tell if the lowlands had had similarly good haymaking weather until the hay arrived.

In her grandfather's time, the hay they made in the high pastures had seen the village livestock through most winters, but the goat herd had grown since then, even more so with Ahab on the council. He'd helped the town prosper, and it had surely grown, so they could sell their surplus down river, but they'd also had to buy in more things they simply didn't have. Without trade, Mirroten would face a hard winter.

But not this winter. Judging by the parade of bundles coming out of the ship's hold, the hayshed beside the town green would be full to the rafters. A good thing, for the harvest from the high pastures had barely filled her own hayloft this year.

Part of her wanted to go down there and see what Mercurio had to sell, but she still had chestnuts to shell, so she fetched a basket and sat down at the table, where she might watch the impromptu market while she worked.

Mercurio's first customer was Tola, carrying two big baskets of herbs to sell. They took their time, bargaining over each item, until Tola looked satisfied. Only then did Tola deign to look at Mercurio's wares, carefully selecting perhaps half a basket's worth of things before any coins changed hands.

Sara smiled. No wonder Mercurio appeared to be sweating – Tola was the one taking the money, not him. Most people didn't know she'd grown up in Rialto, before coming to Mirroten newly widowed, and she'd learned to bargain from the best.

The next customer was Ahab, and his daughter, Ysabel. Sara was surprised to see the girl, for when she'd asked Ahab if Ysabel could help shell nuts, he'd said she was too ill to leave the house. If she'd recovered, Sara should ask again.

She set down her basket and headed down the hill to the lake.

On her way, she met Father Fazzio, the

town priest, carrying a large, cloth-draped bundle.

"Are you selling things to Mercurio, too, Father?" Sara asked.

Fazzio laughed. "No, Mistress Sara. All I have belongs to Mother Church – what would I have to sell? But Mercurio carries goods and messages from my bishop in Rialto, and he is kind enough to transport our messenger birds back." He lifted the cloth to reveal a cage full of pigeons.

Sara blinked. "I thought the point of messenger birds was that they could fly and carry messages on their own. Wouldn't that be faster than sending them by boat?"

Fazzio's eyes widened, before he laughed again. "Oh, yes, of course, but messenger birds only fly home. You cannot train them to fly back and forth, wherever you please. So these birds are Mirroten pigeons, born and raised here. Mercurio will take them to the bishop, who can then send me messages by releasing these pigeons. Ingenious, no?"

Sara had to agree. Before she could say so, however, little Bernard ran up to the priest to breathlessly ask for him to come and help his grandfather. Fazzio promised to speak to Sara more later, and headed off with the boy.

"Mistress Sara! You grow more beautiful with each season that passes!"

She arched her eyebrows. "And your flattery, Master Mercurio, rings even more hollow than last time."

He looked hurt. "Mayhap you cannot see it, but I only speak the truth. Come, Ahab, is Sara not the most beautiful woman alive?"

"Beautiful, but heartless, I fear. I have asked her many a time to marry me, but she still mourns my brother, and will until her dying breath," Ahab replied.

At least that's what she'd told Ahab.

"Heartless, indeed," Mercurio said smoothly. "Any other town along the mighty river, I might find a guest bed in the best house, but Mistress Sara would rather I sleep aboard my cold boat than beneath her roof." His eyes glittered, daring her to defend herself.

But to do so, she'd have to admit she'd taken Mercurio as her lover, after her husband had died, and he'd likely be her lover still, if she hadn't seen him with a maiden in one of the other villages downriver. Well, the girl had been a maiden, until she'd succumbed to the trader's flattery. Sara had no intention of lying with a man who had a mistress in every hamlet he docked at.

"I think only of the virtue of the girls in our town. Your reputation as a seducer of women precedes you, as always, Mercurio." Sara smiled sweetly.

Ahab's eyes grew huge. "Come, Ysabel, we should get started on those mattresses. Even with straw this fresh, they will not stuff themselves." He tugged on his daughter's arm to hurry her back up the hill to town.

Sara almost laughed. Ahab had his shortcomings, but he was absolutely devoted to the protection of his only daughter. Speaking of which…

"Ysabel, I still have chestnuts left to shell. If you have time to help, I can promise you a bag of chestnut flour for the trouble," Sara said.

Ysabel turned. "I thank you for the offer, Aunt Sara, but I must do the mattresses. Maybe when they are finished…"

Sara nodded. "The offer is open until all the nuts are done. At least another week."

Ysabel nodded her thanks, then hurried off in her father's wake.

"What do you have to trade, Mistress Sara? I have much that might interest you. Fine silks from across the sea, candles from the Holy Land you might burn in church to pray for your husband's soul…in fact, I have been fortunate enough to acquire an entire cargo of items from the Holy Land and Byzas. If you ever chose to wear anything but mourning clothes, you might like…" Mercurio flung open a chest, then lifted up a swathe of gossamer thin fabric that shimmered in the sunlight. The sunlight seemed to shine right through the bright stripes, too. "The finest silk from the Far East. You would look divine draped in a dress made of this."

"I'd look like a concubine from someone's harem, more like," Sara said. She shook her head. "Maybe next time you come to Mirroten, Mercurio. The miller has barely begun grinding this year's crop of chestnuts, so I cannot say if we will have any surplus to sell this year. It will still be another week before I'm done shelling them, the harvest was so good. After that, I'd hoped to start on the cheeses, though I'm down a dairyhand since Santina died. No one else can work that kind of magic with milk."

Sadly, Santina had not managed to teach her cheesemaking skills to her daughter Ysabel. They'd both fallen ill of the same summer fever, and only young Ysabel had survived, though she'd been delicate ever since.

Mercurio pressed both hands to his chest. "Argh, but you are heartless indeed, Mistress Sara! Not only do you deny me your warm hospitality, but I do not even have one of your glorious cheeses to sweeten my supper!"

Her cheeses were salty, not sweet at all, but Sara chose not to correct him. Instead, she said, "Perhaps you should try to sell some of your holy candles or other things to Father Fazzio, who has some pigeons for you."

"Perhaps next time, you will feel more kindly disposed toward me, Mistress Sara," Mercurio said.

She couldn't suppress her smile. "Perhaps. It will depend on how good a price you give me for my cheeses."

Mercurio bowed deeply. "Mistress Sara, I have always given you my best, and I always will."

No. No matter how good a lover he'd been, she had no intention of allowing him to share her bed again.

"See you next time, Mercurio." She turned on her heel and headed back up the hill.

Four

"Peace, brother. I mean you no harm."

Zoticus blinked, his bleary eyes focussing on the blade he held at the stranger's throat. The religious brother's throat, judging by the man's tonsured head.

Zoticus sheathed his knife. "Forgive me, brother. What with your dark robes and all, I mistook you for Death, come to claim me."

The monk managed a sad smile. "I suspect Death fears you more than you fear him, for he took everyone else in the village, yet you are still here."

"You mean the plague killed them."

The monk bowed his head. "They no longer suffer, yet by some miracle you have been saved. I must take you to see the Abbot."

Zoticus considered arguing, but this Abbot would likely know more than some lowly monk. "May I have a moment to make myself presentable, then?" he asked instead.

The monk smiled. "Of course. Take all the time you need. I must see if there are any other survivors in the inn."

Zoticus chose not to extinguish the hope in the man's eyes with more truth. Now, if he were travelling with Melisende still, the crusader girl with a magical gift for swiftness, he would have made some wry remark that would make the girl's eyes grow round, the better to drink in all the strange sights as they travelled.

But she was a girl no longer, travelling only occasionally with her husband, for they had several children now. And her brother, the brave but foolish Sir Godfrey…ah, it did not do to dwell on the past.

Particularly when in the present, he needed

to take a piss.

That taken care of, he found a fresh tunic and hose, but what he really wanted was a wash. Heaven only knew how many days he'd lain abed, fighting the plague. Something to ask the Abbot.

What little water remaining in the ewer did not look fresh, so he headed out to the inn yard, in search of a well.

He found a horse trough, the water murkier than the bottom of the jug in his room, and shuddered. The well, when he did find it, was tucked behind the stables, beside the inn's kitchen gardens. Even in the warmth of a summer afternoon, the water felt shockingly cold against his skin.

The vision hit him without warning. The bite of cold air on his cheeks, as a woman dashed across a castle bailey, her heavy cloak flying out behind her like a raven's wings. Her ruddy lips parted as if to speak, urgency darkening her eyes.

Zoticus blinked, and the vision was gone. He knew neither the woman nor her castle, but one day he would stand in that very bailey, witness to the lady's flight. That's how his visions worked.

Several minutes later, washed and dressed in clean garb, he strode out into the town square. Monks carried cloth-wrapped bundles to a cart, before heading back into the cottages where the townspeople had once lived.

A small arm slipped from its wrapping, and Zoticus's blood ran cold. The bundles were all bodies, being taken to the churchyard for burial.

"You should not be here, good sir, if you value your life! Please, I beg you, turn back the way you have come, lest this accursed pestilence take you, too!"

Zoticus spun to face a panicked priest, who seemed to think making shooing motions with his hands would make Zoticus disappear.

"Death didn't want me. One of the monks woke me. I was sleeping in that inn over there." Zoticus pointed.

The priest's eyes widened. He fell to his knees, lifting his face to the sky. "Heavens be praised! A miracle, just as the Abbot predicted!" He fastened his hands on Zoticus's arm. "Sir, you must accompany us back to the Cloister of the Holy Innocents. God himself has saved you, as the Abbot saw in his vision, and you must come!"

Zoticus gently pried his arm free. "You're mistaken, Father. There's nothing holy or miraculous about me. Just a matter of luck, is all." Luck, and magic, but he didn't think this pious priest would want to hear that. "This isn't the first plague I've caught. I went on a crusade once, and our whole ship got sick on the way home. Death doesn't like me, is all."

"Twice saved from the plague…you must be a holy man indeed, sir! I beg you – "

A flash of colour caught Zoticus's eye, and he ignored the priest so he might cross the square to see what it was. One of the bodies had been wrapped in a brightly striped cloak, the sort he'd seen sold in the marketplace in Byzas. The sort crusaders had bought as gifts to take home for sisters, wives, and daughters who would never receive them. Melisende had bought a sack made of the striped stuff, and he'd teased her mercilessly about it. She'd stubbornly hung onto it, until the day of his vision, when those four dishonoured knights had died by his hand.

But the cloak…crusaders had bought every one in the marketplace, until there was no striped cloth left in the whole city. And those who had survived to head home had fallen at the last in the plague ships, their belongings stored in the holds of those doomed vessels.

Ships Zoticus had told Duke Sebastiano to burn, with everything they contained. Surely the man hadn't been foolish enough to take the infected goods and offer them for sale…

But the Duke was a merchant of Rialto. Commerce ran as readily as blood through the veins of a man of Rialto.

Zoticus should have burned the ships with his own hands. Doused them in oil, then thrown a torch in after.

But surely the plague could not persist for more than a decade. He might not be as skilled a healer as his mother or Melisende, but he knew enough about his family's history to be sure. Later, when he was alone, he would sift through the magical memories of his ancestors, to see what else they knew of plagues that might tell him how this could happen.

Yet the cloak wrapped around yet another plague victim shone bright with accusation. He needed to know how a dead crusader's cloak came to be here, of all places, at the same time as a plague slaughtered the town.

"Will you come to the Cloister?" the priest asked. His eyes shone with a kind of fervent faith Zoticus could only envy, for he had never known such a feeling to dwell within his own breast. "It is a most holy place, with relics from the Holy Innocents preserved beneath the altar. I have no doubt it is God's call that woke you from your deathly sleep, calling you to undertake a pilgrimage, sir, to thank God for the miracle of your deliverance!"

Zoticus blinked. Once again, he found himself unwilling to destroy another man's hope. "Perhaps, Father. But first, I must head for Rialto. I have pressing business there, which cannot wait."

Five

When the pony had finished his breakfast, Sara hitched him up to the cart. She'd loaded the last bag of peeled chestnuts last night, and it was time to see whether Regulo had finished milling the previous load. In better times, the answer would have been yes, and he'd have delivered the freshly milled chestnut flour already, but he wasn't the man he'd once been. Perhaps he never would be.

So she walked alongside the plodding pony and cart, as an excuse to see how Regulo and Silvana fared.

"Good morning, Mistress Sara. You're up early!"

She blinked. Father Fazzio looked far too cheerful for such an early hour. Then again, she'd rarely seen him anything less than eager to please.

"My son rises with the sun, and if I am not by the door when he departs, he's likely to forget to take his dinner, and it's a long day in the high pastures for a hungry boy," she said.

He nodded and smiled. "I'm sure my mother thought the same of me. Now I am a man grown, it makes little difference. It is not my mother who seeks to feed me, but most of the mothers in the town, convinced a priest living on his own cannot possibly cook for himself!" He laughed. "They do not believe there were no women in the seminary, and that we were all required to learn to cook. Even if I hadn't, still they give me too much. But that is perhaps a good thing, as then I have surplus to give to the families who need more than they have…" He went on to name names.

Sara only nodded. Between herself and the priest, they saw to it that everyone in town had enough to see them through the winter, and none of the names were news to her.

Then she realised he carried another cloth-draped bundle, much smaller than the one he'd had before.

"Are you bringing breakfast to someone in need, Father?" she asked.

He shook his head. "Oh, no, my messenger pigeons would make a poor meal. Especially this one, which only arrived this morning."

"And what news did he bring from…ah, your bishop, I believe?" Sara asked. She could tell from the slump of his shoulders that it couldn't have been good.

"He sent word of a cursed plague, wiping out the port town of Altino. Not a single man, woman or child was spared," Fazzio said, his eyes wide.

Her heart constricted in her chest. She knew what it meant to lose loved ones to sickness. To lose an entire town… "Oh, that is terrible! All those poor people."

"The bishop cautioned us to remain true to our faith, and not be tempted to wickedness, lest the same fate befall us."

Sara made a rude noise. It wasn't anywhere near as impolite as what she'd say to Fazzio's obnoxious bishop, were he here. "While some of the people of Altino might have been less than virtuous, I cannot believe even the children deserved such a fate. Plagues do not come out of nowhere, and they are spread by people."

"Yet there are cases in scripture that tell us such things have happened in the past. Towns where there was not one good man…"

"I know my scripture, too, Father, and while there may not have been one good man in a particular town, I'm certain there were plenty of good women or at least children. Yet the Bible is mysteriously silent about those."

Father Fazzio seemed nervous at the turn their conversation had taken. Perhaps he feared for his soul. "You are mistaken, Mistress Sara. The Holy Gospel of Saint Matthew clearly tells us that Herod slayed the Holy Innocents, at the time of our Saviour's birth. They are surely saints in heaven, along with all the other martyrs who have given their lives to the Holy Church. Perhaps you should come to the church, to pray to those saints, so that they may strengthen your faith in this dark time." Ah, so it wasn't his soul he feared for, but hers. Perhaps he was right to do so.

Perhaps. If only there was less work to do. She might spare a moment to light a candle, once this delivery was done.

"Will you be heading back to the church soon, Father? Perhaps you might say a prayer for me, and a mass for those poor souls who died in Altino."

He shook his head. "I must bring this pigeon to Mercurio, so he can take it back to the bishop. I pray he has not left yet…" The priest hurried off toward the lake.

Sara shrugged, and continued on to the mill. She might not have hours to spare, on her knees in church, but she could and did pray that Mirroten might be safe from the plague that had afflicted Altino. For it was only a short sail down the river, a thought which sent a cold shiver down her spine.

Please, don't let Mirroten suffer the same fate as Altino.

Six

Rialto had grown since Zoticus had seen it last, as the swampy city always seemed to do. And yet, it grew ever more beautiful as the years passed. He knew plenty of women who would wish to know the city's secret, for their beauty only faded as they gained wisdom.

But if the Duke of Rialto had sold plague goods, then Rialto had descended into the depths of stupidity. No one would buy their trade goods if they were known to be tainted. Surely Sebastiano could not be so senseless.

Unless age had stolen his wits…

At the Ducal Palace, he gave his name to a servant and declined the offer of refreshment, for Duke Sebastiano would not keep him waiting.

Sure enough, Zoticus spotted the servant returning. "His Grace the Duke has no business with you, and he will not see you," the servant said.

"The Duke jests, surely."

The servant shook his head. "The Duke does not jest."

"Duke Sebastiano enjoys a joke as much as I do, I am certain. Take me to him, and you shall see."

The servant stared. "Duke Sebastiano had been dead these last five years. We have a new Duke now."

A cold hand wrapped around Zoticus's heart. Another good man gone. Would he outlive everyone before Death came to claim him?

Zoticus inclined his head. "Then I thank you. I shall visit Palazzo Ziano instead. I imagine Domenico is head of the family now?"

But the servant was already hurrying away.

Zoticus hid his smile. So they did know who he was. Never mind that Zoticus had never killed a man who didn't deserve it – loyal servants were a rare enough breed, without killing them alongside their wayward masters – somehow, his fearsome reputation always preceded him, and made men quake in their boots.

He hoped Sebastiano's sons were as well-informed as the new Duke's servants, or this could be a very tedious trip.

When his boat drew up outside Palazzo Ziano, Zoticus could not help but notice the old water-stained wooden doors had been replaced by shiny new ones clad in bronze. Business had prospered for Sebastiano's family.

Which didn't explain why they'd felt the need to deal in death…

He found two of the sons at home, ensconced in the dining room where he'd shared food and wine with their father. Unlike the new Duke, Domenico and Orso were quick to invite him to join them. Pleased to see that Ziani hospitality had not died with their father, Zoticus was only too happy to take a seat at the table.

"So, did Pietro find you?" Domenico asked, gesturing for a servant to refill Zoticus's wine cup.

"I don't think so," Zoticus said, taking a bite of his fish pie. No one did seafood quite like the cooks of Rialto. "I was taken ill on the road, and when I recovered, I came straight here from Altino."

"Then you must have seen him! He sent a messenger with a chest full of coin from Altino over a week ago, saying he had some final trade negotiations to tie up before he came home."

It seemed Death liked to fondle Zoticus's heart lately, for he felt that cold touch again. "There is no one left in Altino. A plague struck down everyone in the town, leaving nothing but corpses and ghosts. The only people I saw were some monks burying the dead." And insisting he visit their Abbot at his mountain sanctuary, up to and including giving him detailed directions and a map. Memory niggled, and he paled. "It would not surprise me if the monks succumb to the plague, too. I hope your brother's trade negotiations took him far from there." Or Pietro was likely to be dead, too.

Orso raised his cup. "Knowing Pietro, he's probably counting his coins thrice to make sure he was paid properly. Even I can't believe Father forgot about those ships, but Pietro found them and turned a pretty profit on them!"

Was it his imagination, or did the wine taste sour? It had seemed so sweet only a moment before. Zoticus set his cup down. "What ships? What cargo did they carry?"

Domenico shrugged. "These were old ships. Father loaned them to the previous Duke to carry a military force to Byzas or some such place, I believe, but the Duke lost so many men he could not crew all the ships to sail them home, so they remained at Byzas. Shortly before Father died, he sent for his ships, and he anchored them in the lee of one of the shoals at the far end of the lagoon. There they might have remained, had a storm not heaped so much sand on the shoal that it became an island. An island where the Benedictines wanted to build a monastery, but they couldn't, on account of the ships sitting in the sand. The Benedictines wanted to use the timber, for there was a quantity of good oak in those hulls, but the Council would not let them, for they were Ziani ships."

Orso laughed. "You know Pietro. He smelled gold, and he would hear no argument until he had seen those ships. He headed out into the lagoon that very afternoon, and before the day was done, he had an army of men ready to help him dig the ships out of the sand to refloat them, for they were still sound. And their holds were full of cargo that had been sitting there, safe in the sand. The food was spoiled, of course, mostly eaten by rats, and the rats had turned quite savage, with nothing to eat but one another, but he found chests full of cloth and weapons from Byzas. I claimed a chest of silks to send to my sister. She is companion to the Queen in Aros, now."

Ah, yes. Godfrey's bride, Penelope. "If you love your sister, you will burn that chest and everything it contains. I sailed on those ships when they came to Rialto, and plague carried away all those who sailed with me. I told your father to burn the ships, so the pestilence would not spread." Zoticus rose. "On the morrow, I beg you will take me to these ships, so that I may set a torch to them myself."

Domenico shook his head. "It is too late for that. Pietro and his men packed the cargo onto the three most seaworthy ships, and sold the remaining hulks to the Benedictines. He sold the cargo before he reached Altino, for he sent the coin home. The chests are in the strongroom even now, waiting for Pietro to return and take it to our bankers."

Pietro would not return. Zoticus knew it as surely as he knew more innocent people would die if he did not burn what remained of that cargo and the ships carrying it.

And it would be his fault.

"If Pietro or any of that cargo comes here, you keep it away from everyone else until I return. I'll buy everything from you, I swear, and I'll pay any fair price for it. If you place any value in the friendship I had with your father, with your family, you will let me do this," Zoticus said.

Orso's eyes widened. "I did not know the assassination trade was so profitable."

It wasn't the profit, so much as the number of commissions he'd taken in a long and successful career, coupled with how little he'd spent over the years. Years of bringing death to those who deserved it, for deeds even he did not want to speak of, and he would hand over every copper coin he'd ever earned to deny death an even bigger harvest at his hand.

Zoticus wet his lips. "I assure you I have gold enough to satisfy even you."

"Father's account books say that though the ships are his, the cargo aboard them belonged to you. Pietro said he would search for you, while we kept your portion of the proceeds in our strongroom. The coin is yours to do with as you please, including buy ships, if that is your wish. Rialto-built ships are the best merchant vessels afloat, and rarely sold to men who are not citizens of our fair city, but as Father trusted you with our ships in the past, so will we in the future."

Breath whooshed out of his lungs – relief,

though fleeting. There was still much to be done. "Thank you. If you will tell me where Pietro went, and where he planned to go, perhaps that will speed up my search."

"Finding him would place us in your debt," Domenico said.

Zoticus inclined his head. "Consider it a favour, as a friend."

"Only if you sup with us tonight, and remain as a guest in our house until the morrow. In the morning, we will furnish you with a boat and a crew, to help you with your search."

Zoticus sat down. "Gladly. If you do business so smoothly with everyone, I suspect you will soon be the richest merchants in Rialto, if you are not already."

Orso winked. "Perhaps."

Zoticus settled in for a pleasant evening, smiling and laughing with the two men he hoped would never know how many times he'd been asked to dispose of members of their family, though he'd refused every time. The richer they became, the more enemies they created.

Yes, the Ziani brothers had been partially responsible for the plague outbreak in Altino, but these two had not known the risks carried by that fateful cargo. Not like he or their father had. But with Sebastiano dead, the blame fell squarely on his shoulders.

This time, he swore, he would save people instead of killing them.

Seven

By the time Tobias returned home that evening, Sara had spoken to Tola and Gojko the apothecary, and she'd spent the rest of the day attempting to implement all the plague prevention measures she'd learned.

Both his bed and hers were stuffed with fresh hay from the high pastures, mixed liberally with pennyroyal, lady's bedstraw and rosemary. Swanhild had brought her a basket of fresh sage, which they'd both hung in bunches from the rafters to dry.

She'd bought every health-promoting herb,

tea and potion they'd had on hand, urging both Tola and Gojko to make as many as they could, in preparation for a possible plague.

Mercurio had left, so Regulo had his millhands back at work again, and Silvana had promised to bring up a load of flour as soon as the cart was full.

Beorma the brewer had sent over three casks of cider vinegar, and promised a dozen more when he'd finished brewing this season's crop of cider apples. A good thing, too, for she'd used most of the first cask cleaning everything in the house, and now she could smell nothing but vinegar.

"What is that smell?" Tobias asked, wrinkling his nose.

He likely smelled of grass from the high pastures, and the mountain air. Healthy air, free of sickness, if Tola was to be believed.

"It is the smell of cleaning. A plague came to Altino, and many people died. I cleaned the house because Tola said good hygiene helps to stop sickness." Sara wrung her hands. "She also said oranges and lemons would help, but she had not seen any since leaving Rialto.

Father Fazzio suggested all we need to do is pray, to stay safe, but surely that is not enough, or someone in Altino might have been saved. You must go only to the high pastures, and come straight home at night, too, for the fewer people you see, the less chance you can catch the plague. Oh, I should ask Ahab to call a special council meeting, so we can discuss how we shall protect the town!"

"There is no plague here, Mother, and perhaps it is not so bad in Altino. They're all the way down the river, by the sea. You've told me yourself that sometimes stories can grow bigger in the telling than they ever were in life…" He reached out and took her hands. By all that was holy, he was beginning to look like his father. "It won't be that bad. You worry too much."

She squeezed his hands, then let go. "Perhaps I worry more than I should. But I'm your mother – it's what mothers do. And, since I lost your father, you're all I have. If I lost you, I'm not sure what I would do."

He grinned. "Well, you're not going to lose me, so that's one thing you won't have to worry about. Soon I'll be a man, and I'll be able to take your place on the council, and you won't have to worry about that, either."

It was his Uncle Ahab's place he would take on the council, not hers, but she didn't say that. Ahab had only joined the council after his brother's death, while she grieved his loss. When she'd surfaced from her grief and Tobias had been old enough for her to attend council meetings, she'd been grateful that Ahab had stayed. Tobias should start attending the meetings soon, so he'd get to know what happened. Soon. When the plague had passed.

"Just…promise me you will keep yourself safe, stay away from anyone in town who appears ill, and spend as much time as possible in the clean, mountain air," Sara said.

Tobias laughed. "You forgot to remind me to watch out for the goats."

She managed a smile. "Well, yes. You've been goatherd long enough, I thought you might have grasped that by now."

"It's been years since I lost one, and I still hold that the kid wasn't moving at all when the eagle carried it off. It might have been already dead."

"Yes, well…"

"What's for supper?"

Poor Tobias, always hungry.

"I've been so busy cleaning today, I almost forgot to cook. Luckily, old Matteo caught more fish than he could eat out on the lake today, so I've made a fish stew and there's fresh bread…"

While she ate supper with her son, at least she didn't have to worry about him not eating enough. Two helpings, and he looked like he was considering a third…

Eight

The raven-winged woman flew through Zoticus's dreams that night. The panic in her eyes set his heart racing, as if he shared her fears.

So, it couldn't be him she feared, though she looked right at him. Something she was fleeing from, maybe…

In the vision, Zoticus focussed on what was behind her. A stone castle, yes, but it was built into the side of a hill. No, more like a mountain, for he could see snow-capped peaks towering into the distance behind the castle.

Not here, then. His vision would not happen today.

Zoticus blew out a breath. None of his visions had ever affected him so much before. He'd long since learned that they were glimpses of a future he could not change, and they only grew clearer as the event he'd seen approached. So why did this one feel so urgent?

Perhaps she was a possible plague victim he had to save. But pestilence was not something she could run from…and he was not some noble knight, or someone who could work miracles.

Except his own recovery from the plague, which was no miracle, no matter what that monk had believed.

He rose, wishing for just a moment that he could spend every night in a fine feather bed, like the Ziani family did. But the mattress alone would not fit into his travelling bags.

He had two travelling bags — a sack that seemed to carry all his belongings, and a small, rough pouch scarcely large enough to contain his midday meal, had it not been magically enhanced. He spread the pouch flat on his bed, where it looked like little more than a ragged circle two handspans across. An empty circle, which yet contained enough gold to buy Sebastiano's ships, weapons and clothing to let him travel comfortably anywhere in the world, and an assortment of other magical objects that had come in useful on more than one occasion. Moreover, most of them could only be used by someone who had his blood. Well, more accurately, his mother's blood, for she was the powerful enchantress who had enchanted all his things, but because she was his mother, her blood ran through his veins and allowed him to use the items as though he possessed a measure of his sister's or his mother's magic. He was nowhere near as powerful as either of them, of course – Zoraida had singlehandedly fought a dragon! – but it gave him an edge, and kept him alive.

He stretched his hand out over the splayed pouch, thinking about what he would need for his quest.

His quest to find the plague ships and the goods they contained, and perhaps Pietro, too.

He'd need a light cloak, yet something tightly woven enough to keep the weather off, and keep him warm at night.

The corner of a striped Byzas cloak appeared in his hand. Zoticus laughed softly. He'd forgotten he had it – a gift given to him by Godfrey, who'd complained that Zoticus wore too much grey. He still wasn't sure if Godfrey had known he was an assassin.

Then again, this quest was about saving lives, not taking them, so perhaps he should wear another colour than grey. When he burned the ships and their cargo, he would wear the silly striped cloak.

But in the meantime, he'd need another cloak, some more clothes, his healing amulet…

When he'd packed all the necessary items into his travelling sack, and made himself look presentable for the day, he tied the pouch to his belt again, and headed down to break his fast.

He found Domenico and Orso already in the dining chamber. Once more, he wondered if he was mistaken. Had they knowingly sold tainted goods, for a bit of extra gold? Or was this all a matter of Pietro's greed, which he had likely already paid the price for?

"I hope you find him, and succeed in finding those ships," said Domenico, almost as if he shared his sister's talent for reading minds.

Zoticus did not need such a talent – he knew truth from lies, and Domenico meant every word. Zoticus relaxed. If the Ziani brothers had been responsible for spreading the plague, he would have been honour bound to return and exact justice from them. As it was, he strongly suspected he would never see these men again.

He ate a few bites, before bidding them both thanks and farewell.

Domenico walked down to the dock with him, pressing a sizeable sack of supplies into his hands for the journey.

Zoticus boarded the small sailing boat, exchanging nods with the two men who crewed her, and with a push of a pole, they were out in the middle of the canal, and Zoticus's quest had truly begun.

He only prayed it would come to a

satisfactory end.

Nine

It looked like most of the town had turned up for the council meeting. Even Tobias was there, though he was hiding in the back with Raphael, the apothecary's apprentice, as if he didn't want her to see him.

But she hadn't the heart to send him home, no matter how much she feared for his safety. He deserved to hear all they knew about the plague, and what the council planned to do about it. If he had questions or even suggestions, she'd see that they were heard. She might not sit in the place of honour — that belonged to Ahab – but even from her end of the high table, she would be heard, if she chose to speak up.

Not that she'd need to. The people of Mirroten were a sensible lot, most of the time.

Ahab called for quiet, and the chattering crowd obeyed. He cleared his throat, then said, "I've called you all here to hear some grave news Father Fazzio has received from his bishop. It's best that Father Fazzio tell you himself."

The priest, seated at Ahab's right hand, rose. "The port of Altino has been afflicted with plague."

A low murmur rose from the crowd, though not loud enough to drown out Fazzio's words as he filled in what details he had. None that Sara did not already know, so she let her gaze drift over the crowd.

Tola wasn't there, and nor were some of the frailer members of the town. Most of the children were in bed by now, so there were few young people present, except for Tobias and Raphael, who'd been joined by Swanhild and Silvana.

"What happens if it comes here, too?"

Sara couldn't see who had spoken, but it did not matter.

Everyone looked worried.

"What shall we do?" was the cry on everyone's lips as they turned to each other in panic.

Sara found herself rising to her feet, her hands out to placate them all. "We are quite a way upriver from Altino, so if we stay here, and avoid contact with anyone who has been to the tainted town, we should be safe. We are well provisioned for the winter, and there is much left to harvest before the first snows fall. If we forgo all trade with towns closer to the coast, we will all see next summer safely. Meanwhile, if you find yourself ill, speak to Tola or Gojko, who know many remedies that will soon see you back in good health. There is nothing to worry about." She tucked her skirts beneath her and sat down.

In the silence that followed, she found the townsfolk nodding, looking relieved. She might not be a leader like Ahab or even her late husband, but the people trusted her to do what was right.

"Of course there is nothing to worry about. Altino was a den of wickedness, full of sailors and infidels and thieves. Mirroten is a beacon of virtue compared to the likes of them! But we cannot forgo trade. What Mistress Sara forgets is that we only have winter fodder because Mercurio brought it on his boat, not even a week ago. And the herbs and medicines Tola and Gojko sell? Also bought from Mercurio! Trade is the lifeblood of our town, and we cannot stop it, any more than we can stop our own hearts from beating without committing a mortal sin.

"What does your bishop advise us to do, so that we do not share the same fate as Altino?" Ahab boomed.

Fazzio didn't even glance at Sara. "The Bishop commands us to stay on the true path. To lead virtuous lives, so we do not invite God's wrath upon us. We should…pray, and never close our doors to those who might seek our assistance or hospitality. Because as His Most Holy Son said in the Gospels, whoever welcomes the least of his flock, welcomes the

Lord himself into their home."

Sara bowed her head. She'd offer charity to any member of Mirroten, rich or poor, but to a stranger who might carry the plague and kill them all? Did God really require that of her?

Ahab pounded on the table. "And there you have it. We cannot close off our town to the outside world. God himself forbids it. We will pray, and we shall trade, and we shall stand out as a beacon of virtue in the mountains that will shine out to the very sea itself, so that other towns between us and Altino will know how to save themselves, too."

No. That couldn't be right. Sara opened her mouth to say so.

Someone let out a cheer, and soon the whole hall was filled with happily cheering townsfolk. Any words that might have left Sara's lips were drowned out by their pre-emptive cries of triumph.

A hand landed heavily on her shoulder.

Sara jumped out of her seat, only to find Ahab behind her.

"Next time, stay silent, and you will not look so foolish," he said gently. "You know little about what it takes to run a town, and as a woman, your soft heart will lead you astray. Remember, Adam would be safe in Eden had Eve not tempted him with the apple, after she had surrendered to temptation. You only have a place on this council out of respect to your father. If you lose the respect of the townspeople through further foolishness, you will lose your seat on the council, too. Leave leadership to your betters." Another pat, and he left.

Sara squeezed her eyes shut. She would not let them see her cry. She wouldn't.

Yes, she'd been foolish to speak first. She should have waited, and then spoken her piece. That it had taken Ahab, the son of a goatherder, to point out what she should have seen by herself, rankled the most.

Next time, she would not make the same mistake. She would do everything in her power to save this town, and no amount of condescension would stop her. She would be better.

Next time.

Ten

"There! Do you see those three ships, anchored in that cove? Can you get us closer?" It had been years since he'd boarded one, but Zoticus would recognise those ships anywhere. You didn't forget the floating coffin that had very nearly been your final resting place.

Viator, the owner of the small sailing boat, nodded. Then he turned to his nephew. "Fidelis, take us around the headland."

Zoticus kept out of their way as the two men turned their boat away from Altino to enter the eastern cove instead. When the nearest ship was close enough he hailed it: "Ho, the ship!"

He tried several times, but nothing moved on deck. The same with the second ship. And the third…

"That isn't a Ziani vessel," Viator said, jerking his head at the third, smaller ship. "That's a river trading boat."

"That's Mercurio's boat," Fidelis agreed.

All three of them shouted for Mercurio, to no avail.

The two sailors looked worried, so Zoticus volunteered, "I'll go aboard, to see if there is anyone there. Or some clue to where they might have gone." He didn't dare give voice to what they were all thinking – that nothing but ghosts sailed these ships now. "I'll meet you on the shore over there." He pointed at a tiny beach.

He stripped down to his tunic, then dived over the side. Though it was still summer, the water was colder than he would have liked. The brisk swim to Mercurio's boat kept him warm, though, and the air did not chill his skin when he climbed aboard.

A swift search soon revealed that the river boat was empty. No goods worth trading, and no dead bodies, either. The other two ships were much the same – no more than a couple of empty water barrels between them. The ships, however, had dead rats floating in the bilge beneath the empty hold.

Zoticus swore. Hard though it was to believe that these ships and cargo had carried the plague for years before spreading it to Altino, the evidence was right here before his eyes.

But where was the third ship, and all the cargo? Not to mention Pietro and the mysterious Mercurio.

The answers, he hoped, lay in Altino, where they would sail next when he rejoined the fishing boat. Too late, he realised he should have asked them to keep their distance, lest the beach be tainted, too. His only hope was to reach it before them, so that he might warn Viator to stay offshore.

He dived into the water once more, stroking for the shore. He didn't stop until the sand crunched beneath his bare feet and it was shallow enough for him to stand. He turned to see that by some trick of the weather, the wind had died down, and he'd beaten the becalmed boat to shore.

"Stay there! The beach might be tainted. I'll swim to you once I'm done taking a closer look," Zoticus shouted.

Viator nodded and said something to Fidelis. A moment later, Fidelis dropped the anchor.

Zoticus let out a breath. They were safe. For it soon became apparent that this beach was far from it.

Above the high tide line sat several torn sacks, their contents spilling out onto the sand, with more rat corpses half-buried in the spoiled grain and flour. From here, Zoticus spied a track that led away from the water. His feet felt leaden as they led him along the track, which soon widened until two wagons could travel along it, side by side, as the wheel tracks showed they had done. Sand dunes and beach scrub gave way to fields of stubble – harvested within the last few weeks, if Zoticus was not mistaken. Likely hay for winter fodder, though it was safe in someone's barn now.

More rat bodies lay between the shorn tussocks, and an eagle eyed him suspiciously, before spreading her wings in an impressive mantle and resuming her meal of decayed rat. There were no dead birds in the field, Zoticus noticed. Perhaps they did not succumb to the plague as readily as rats and humans. He hoped so, for the eagle's sake.

He followed the road to the top of a rise, and drew in a sharp breath. Altino lay spread out before him, beside the rippled river. Fishing boats lined up along the canals, but there was no sign of life. Not even a curl of smoke from someone's cookfire. Even the monks had gone.

Monks who had given him directions to their monastery, and multiple invitations to visit. Zoticus still didn't understand their vehemence. Maybe the Abbot had wanted to engage his services as an assassin, for he could not think of any other reason the man might need him, imagined miracles notwithstanding.

Something to consider after this current quest was complete.

He headed back to the boat, hoping his swim would be enough to wash any pestilence off his clothes and body. Just in case, he warned Viator and Fidelis to keep their distance from him until he'd washed properly and changed into clean garb. His wet tunic went over the side into the water – better to buy another one than risk infecting anyone else. He'd use his healing amulet on himself when darkness fell, to banish any hint of disease in his blood.

But first, he had to burn the ships.

He strung his Seljuk longbow with care, before slipping on the worn finger guard that no one would think to look twice at. Anyone who could not sense the spell on the old leather, anyway. Next, he pulled four arrows from his quiver, each wrapped in a piece of cloth. The slosh of liquid told him none of them had broken yet, though they would soon. These particular hollow shafts were crafted to shatter on impact, showering the target in Greek fire, a substance so flammable, the Church had declared it a mortal sin to use the stuff in battle. He risked excommunication by even possessing it, though he knew no pope would ever dare to do so. There were cardinals aplenty who would pay handsomely for an assassin to bring the Pope's reign to an end.

Even the Seljuk bow should not have been able to fire the heavy arrows across the water to the ships, but that was where the magic finger guard came in – when he wore it, his every shot would find its target, though it helped if he was a decent shot to start with. Magic could only do so much.

He fired two arrows at each ship, far enough apart to spatter the decks in the oily fluid. A final pair of fire arrows finished the job, like orange shooting stars arcing across the water, before they kissed the Greek fire.

Flames raced across the decks of both ships, lighting up the sky more brightly than the sunset in the west. A friendly night breeze blew the smoke away from their boat, so they sat down to watch the ships' final fate as they ate their evening meal.

The burning deck of the first ship collapsed into the hold, taking the mast and reefed sails with it. This was more than the ship's hull could take, for it careened over on its side, revealing a hold that could easily have been mistaken for the gate to hell, before it slipped beneath the water.

Sparks from the fire on the second ship set some of its ropes alight, freeing the sail. The night breeze caught the sail and the second boat heeled over, too, still burning brightly, until it, too, sank.

That left only Mercurio's trading boat and themselves in the cove.

Inevitably, their talk turned to the missing ship.

"It could be anywhere. Any of the port cities along the coast. That's a Rialto merchant galley, the best trading vessel in the world," Fidelis said.

Viator's brow creased as he chewed thoughtfully on a piece of dried fish.

"Pietro said he would remain in Altino, to finalise a deal of some sort. Wherever it went, it left from here, likely before the plague took hold in the town. But before or after the harvest?" Zoticus mused.

"After." Viator took a swig from the jug of

wine, then set it down. "Altino and all the coastal towns here send extra hay upriver to the mountain towns, to feed their animals through the winter. Mercurio spends all autumn making his way up and down the river, trading hay and dried fish for the bounty in the mountains. Goat cheeses so sweet you'd swear they were soaked in honey. Chestnut smoked bacon, like nothing else you've ever tasted. And bags of the nuts themselves, to roast upon the fire. Anything worth trading, Mercurio will find the value in it. He will know where your cargo is, and maybe your missing ship, too."

"If he's still alive, and hasn't succumbed to the plague," Zoticus said, debating whether to stuff meat or cheese into his flatbread. He opted for both. His first satisfying bite told him he'd made the right decision. He looked up to find both men staring at him. "What?"

"Is this plague truly so deadly?" Fidelis asked.

Zoticus swallowed. He wished he could make light of things, but they deserved to know the risks they faced. "All of the people in

Altino are dead. If Pietro or Mercurio were there, it is likely they died, too. I saw the town from the road that leads to the beach. No movement, no smoke…no life. This plague is like nothing else I have known. There is no cure, and everyone I know who has caught it died of it."

Viator squinted at him. "Except you. Master Orso said you were saved."

Death did not want him. Not yet. But Zoticus dared not tell these men about his visions. "Magic saved me. I have a magical amulet a witch gave me. It protects me. I am still afflicted by disease, like anyone else, but I will not die of it."

Viator nodded. "So it's both a blessing and a curse. A wise witch, whoever gave it to you."

Zoticus laughed. "She is my mother, and I thank you for the compliment. She is wiser than I will ever be. I'm sure she would find this missing ship, and our men, too."

"If Mercurio has it, then he has taken it upriver to trade. We could try following him tomorrow. Not before first light, though, for the river has some treacherous shallows for those that don't know it, much like the shoals around Rialto. It's been years since I've been further inland than Altino, but I'll take you as far as I can," Viator said.

It was as good a guess as any, so Zoticus agreed. It felt right, and he wasn't a man who ignored his intuition.

And it took him into the mountains, where he might meet this woman who haunted his dreams.

Yes, upriver they would go.

Eleven

Towns and villages slipped by as they sailed upriver, each as silent and smokeless as Altino. More than once, he'd caught Fidelis and Viator crossing themselves, murmuring prayers and muttering about ghosts. Even Zoticus had felt the spirits of the newly dead staring at him through the ether, all accusing him of coming too late.

He'd gone ashore at the first three towns, before the stench of death had sickened him too much to do it again.

The dead villagers might not be capable of

answering his questions, but they told him enough. The plague had passed through their village, and then swept on up the river, pushed by the sails of the third cursed ship.

It was enough to make him want to weep. So many innocent lives lost, because one greedy merchant had not burned the boats like he'd asked him. Because one careless assassin had left them with that merchant to report that he'd succeeded in killing more men. And he'd saved a horse.

Stupid, foolish…the words he could have heaped on his own head for his folly would never be enough, for they could never restore the lives that had been lost.

"There it is," Fidelis breathed.

"Thank Heaven for small mercies. The ship never reached Mirroten," Viator said.

"What's Mirroten?" Zoticus asked.

Viator pointed. "A short sail further on, there is a great lake. Mirroten is the town on the lakeshore. The people earn their livelihood from the mountains. Many medicinal herbs are only found here, and the chestnut groves grow wonderfully well. And the cheeses…they say it's the mountain pastures, making for finer milk than the lowlands, but my sister says there's old magic here. She should know. She's the town witch." There was pride in his voice at that.

"So once we've dealt with this ship, we can go into town and visit your sister?" Zoticus suggested.

Viator shook his head. "She has not spoken to any of our family for many years. My father forced her to marry a man whose wickedness…ah, if only I'd known. When he drank too much wine, he beat her. One night, he was so drunk he fell in a canal and drowned. She disappeared the same night. At first, we thought her dead, too, but some of her things were gone from the house. Things she would never leave behind.

"I searched for years, until I heard a whisper about a new witch in Mirroten. I sailed up here myself to see, and she threatened to turn me into a fish and cook me for dinner if I ever returned, or breathed a word to our father that she'd survived. She had a child, too, a little girl who looked just like her. So, no, I will not be welcome in Mirroten, though you may have better luck."

Zoticus nodded. He hadn't seen his sister in years, either, though he knew she'd had children with her husband. She'd probably have set fire to her husband if he'd tried to beat her, though. She'd fought a dragon once and lived, which was more than most men could say.

Fidelis hailed the ship. After the river of death they'd sailed through, Zoticus would have been surprised to hear a response. Of course, there wasn't one.

"Bring me as close as you can, then stand off a ways. I'll swim back," Zoticus said.

Viator did as he asked, and Zoticus soon pulled himself over the gunwales of the missing ship. And swore.

The hold was full, with more casks stacked on deck. A lumpy pallet covered in a striped cloak took most of the leftover space, and the stench coming from it didn't bode well.

Zoticus swallowed, then forced himself to step forward and snatch up the cloak. The corpse beneath it could not have been dead for more than a day, but the summer heat had not been kind. It wasn't Pietro, so he assumed it was Mercurio, the lost river trader.

Pietro must have perished in Altino, like he'd originally thought.

Fidelis shouted his name, and Zoticus moved to the side of the ship, where the others could see him.

"Have you found them?"

Zoticus wet his lips. "We were too late. They're both dead." Not technically a lie, but he had no intention of letting the two fishermen aboard to see for themselves. "We should return to Rialto, to tell Domenico and Orso that their brother is dead."

"What about my sister?" Viator seemed surprised at his own outburst.

If it was Zoraida, Zoticus wouldn't have hesitated to see for himself. But the plague posed little danger to him, while it could be deadly to Viator and his nephew.

"I'll go up to the town and see if she is well." Zoticus wasn't a praying man, but he was willing to pray for Viator's sister's health. "How long will it take for me to reach the town?"

"Half a mile along the shore, so not long at all. But if Tola is well, she will surely offer you hospitality you cannot refuse. It'll be days before she lets you leave, and only then because you fear you will be sick from eating so much." Viator laughed, but it sounded forced. "If not…"

"If she is ill, then I will do my best to heal her," Zoticus promised. At best, all he could do would be to ease her passing, but that was something, at least. "Go to Rialto. I will meet you there, or send word if I cannot."

Viator clasped his hands together and bowed. "You do me a great service, Master Zoticus. If ever you have need of a fisherman, or a boat, or anything at all, come to me in Rialto. I will leave your things on the riverbank, near the road to town. May God continue to preserve you!"

Preserves. That gave Zoticus an idea. He checked all the casks on deck until he found one that contained lamp oil. Not as effective as Greek fire, but it would still burn, and he could save the stronger stuff for another time.

He splashed the oil across the deck, on the corpse, and as much of the cargo as he could reach. Noises from a cloth-draped bundle made him put the cask down and investigate further. Beneath the cloth was a cage of messenger pigeons, still alive.

He'd seen plenty of dead people on the way here, but not a single dead bird. Perhaps the pigeons, like the eagle in Altino, truly were immune to the plague. He could not stand to burn the birds alive, either, so he opened the cage and let them fly free. They all headed in the same direction – toward the lake.

His next destination, too.

When he ran out of oil, Zoticus leaped over the side of the ship and into the water. The river current was slow here, so it was an easy swim to shore, where Viator had left his sack and his bow. Ah, yes, he would send a fire arrow into this ship, too, and stay until it sank into the river. Only then would this quest be over, so that he might start the new one to see to Viator's sister.

Twelve

Walking into a town with living, breathing people was a surreal experience. He'd seen so much death in the last few days that life seemed too loud. Breathing in the smells of cooking and smoke without the miasma of death made Zoticus almost light-headed.

"Are you well, sir?"

He looked up to meet the eyes of a concerned man. A farm labourer, or Zoticus missed his guess. A commoner who could not tell the difference between a knight and an assassin, but sensed deference would serve him best.

Zoticus wet his lips. "I soon will be, if you could direct me to a witch, or herb-woman, if you have one in this town."

The man's chest puffed out. "Here in Mirroten, we have our own apothecary. You can't miss his house – there is the sign of the mortar and pestle over the door."

Zoticus managed a thin smile. "But I want to see the witch."

"Oh." The man shrugged, before some thought occurred to him that creased his face with suspicion. He squinted at Zoticus. "I hope you don't mean to bring trouble to our town. Mirroten looks after its own, and no mistake. But if it is truly our witch you want, you will find Mistress Tola's house three doors down from the apothecary."

Zoticus thanked the man and continued down the road. Sure enough, he spotted the crudely carved bowl with a stick over the door of the apothecary, but he continued walking.

He smelled the witch's house before he saw it, for she had bunches of herbs strung up to dry beneath the eaves of her cottage. Sage, mostly, but there were rare mountain flowers hiding amid all the leaves. Perhaps he should pretend his business here was herbs, and not mention Viator at all. He'd been meaning to stock up on a few things, anyway, and here was the ideal opportunity.

He raised a hand and knocked on the door. When he received no answer, he pushed the door open and stuck his head inside. "Hello, is the healer home?" He waited a moment, then stepped into the house.

"No, but I am," said a young, feminine voice.

Zoticus blinked. A girl stood on the other side of a counter, her hands on her hips. No longer a child, but not quite a woman, either. Likely Viator's niece, if he was not mistaken.

He bowed. "My pardon, mistress. Perhaps you could tell me where I might find the healer?"

She smiled, an enchanting sight that likely would have half the male population of this town swooning at her feet. "Well now, seeing as you mean me no harm, perhaps I can help you. I know as much as my mother when it comes to healing, maybe more, depending on your ailment." She looked him up and down, as if searching for sickness.

Perhaps she was. He could sense the magic in her blood, though he wasn't sure what shape her gift took.

A vision hit him, of this girl flapping her arms and crying out, before transforming into a swan. He blinked, and he was back in the cottage again.

"If it is the falling sickness you suffer from, sir, then I recommend rue. I have some fresh leaves from which you can make an infusion, or you can buy it powdered for tea, but you might prefer a vial of oil of rue, which is easier to use for a traveller like yourself. I've made a fresh batch just this week, in preparation for autumn coughs and colds, but it is good for the falling sickness, too. Just a drop in the morning after you break your fast…"

She'd seen him freeze as the vision took him, and mistaken it for illness instead of magic. What she did not know was that rue only intensified the visions.

Then another thought struck him.

"How do you know I mean you no harm?" he demanded.

She smiled again. "Because if you did, the enchantment on the door would have turned you into a frog."

So her mother's threat to Viator hadn't been an empty one. "Your mother can transform people into animals?" He'd heard of a family line in the mountains who passed such a gift down the generations. Perhaps Tola was descended from them.

The girl's face twisted. "When she was a girl, yes, but my father tried to beat the magic out of her, so now her magic is not as strong as it was. The door enchantment will only make you believe you are a frog, and you'll behave like one for a day or two, before returning to normal. That's how she escaped my father – she made him think he was a fish."

And he'd drowned in a Rialto canal.

"Then I must speak to your mother. Can you tell me where I can find her, please?"

The girl sighed. "She took some oil of rue up to Elder Ahab's house. His daughter's always been sickly, and she's ailing again. Poor

Ysabel."

Zoticus nodded. "So I should look for the biggest, grandest house, and that's where I'll find her?"

She burst out laughing. "Heavens, no! Well, you might, for Mother and Sara are great friends, but Ahab's house is behind the meeting hall, beside the town green. His family has the rights to use the cottage as long as they repair the fences around the green. You should have heard him swearing when they all blew over in that spring storm a couple of years back!"

The girl would make a good village witch, when the time came. She knew all the town gossip, without revealing anything about herself – he still didn't know what her magical gifts were, or even her name.

"So I will find Mistress Tola at the cottage behind the meeting hall, next to the town green?" he asked.

"Oh, for certain. Unless she has already seen to Ysabel and there is a town council meeting. In fact, I remember her saying there might be a meeting. Maybe then she'll be in the meeting hall."

Zoticus shook his head. So much for certainty. Then again, in a town this small, finding anyone wouldn't be that hard. As long as they were still alive, though that seemed likely.

"Thank you," he said. "You have been most helpful."

"Are you sure you don't want some oil of rue to take with you? You won't get it any fresher, and the price will only go up with winter on the way."

The girl was a witch, but she had the blood of a Rialto merchant in her veins, of that he was certain. Almost against his will, he found himself pulling out his purse. "How much?"

Thirteen

"We need to do more to encourage traders to come here. Now they no longer stop in Altino, traders will come up the river in search of what we can provide. The more people know about our products, the more they will want them! Instead of one trader, we should have a dozen traders, maybe more, sailing up and down the river to take our goods for sale in the markets of Rialto. Better yet, we should send invitations to all the merchants of Rialto, inviting them here for some sort of celebration, so they can see all we can offer, and they can show their wares to us." Ahab's grin beamed around the hall, seeking encouragement to continue. He wanted this so much, and it sounded so promising, even Sara wondered if maybe…

She could see Tola shaking her head.

Someone had to stop him, and now seemed a good moment. "Perhaps after this plague outbreak is over, then we might send someone to Rialto to meet with the merchants," Sara ventured. "Someone who has all of the town's interests in mind. But now, with just Mercurio, we didn't have enough trade goods to fill his new ship. He'll have to return in the autumn, when we have more to sell. With the news of plague in Altino and maybe other places, too, we cannot be too careful. Allowing new people into the town now may bring the pestilence here."

"And who is better equipped to deal with sickness than a healthful place like Mirroten? Why, we have more healing herbs here than anywhere else in the world, I'm certain of it! Why else would Mercurio buy so much from us? We are good, pious people, not steeped in sin like some port full of sailors and unspeakable things. God would never visit a plague on us!"

Oh, by all that was holy…when he started invoking religion, she had no hope of swaying anyone to her side. She'd learned that lesson last meeting. But she had to try. They could not risk…

"Actually, the lady is right. The plague took every soul in Altino, saint and sinner alike. And every town along the river between here and the lagoon. This wasn't God's doing. This was a trader, selling tainted goods to those towns. You're lucky he never reached you, or your people would be dying, too."

Sara stared at owner of the voice. He strode into the hall like he owned it, muscles bulging as he folded his arms across his fine linen tunic. A Rialto merchant, maybe, or some neighbouring lord. A handsome stranger she needed to know more about.

"And who are you?" Ahab asked, bristling like an alarmed hedgehog.

The stranger delivered a courtly bow so practiced, Sara was certain he'd spent time in a royal court. "I am Master Zoticus, and I have come to save your town from the plague."

No title. Not a prince or a lord or a baron or even a knight. Master Zoticus, indeed.

Sara smelled a rat. "At what cost, Master Zoticus? What price must we pay for your services?"

He bowed deeper still. "I would do it simply for the pleasure of serving you, my lady."

Ahab spluttered incoherently.

Anyone who could render Ahab speechless and support her in keeping Mirroten safe could not be all bad.

For the first time that day, Sara flashed a brilliant smile at the newcomer. She was almost embarrassed to hear her voice come out in a low purr as she said, "Then, Master Zoticus, I accept."

He straightened and his eyes met hers. She could not look away, and nor could he, it seemed. Perhaps she imagined the startled look in his eyes, for it was gone almost as soon as it had appeared.

Then, as swiftly as he had entered the hall, he turned on his heel, and was gone.

Fourteen

The woman in his vision. The sight of her had unnerved him for a moment, but Zoticus was certain no one had noticed. She hadn't appeared the slightest bit perturbed, let alone panicked, and on this warm summer evening, she wore no cloak. Her voice had been delightfully warm, too…

He stopped that thought before it blossomed into something far more troublesome. He'd met many beautiful women, and he'd never let his lust for them get in the way of getting a job done. Currently, she was his client, which made his attraction to her even easier to ignore. Because if he didn't complete this quest, she might die of the plague.

But not before he'd seen the panic in her eyes as her mourning cloak flew behind her.

Which meant someone close to her would die, as she wasn't wearing mourning now.

He had to concentrate on his mission, not some mystery woman.

He found the town's only inn, and the innkeeper allowed him to rent a room if, "You promise not to tell Mistress Sara. She was most particular about not having strangers to stay."

In a town this small, Mistress Sara and anyone else who cared would know he was staying in the inn within a day, but Zoticus merely smiled and gave the woman his word.

The room was larger than the one in Altino, and a lot cleaner, too. This wasn't a town that saw too many visitors, and right now, he was the sole guest at the inn, which suited him fine. He paid extra to have his supper brought up to him, instead of joining the townsfolk in the taproom. Their curiosity about him would not save them from the plague.

Only when the maid had taken away his empty supper dish did he start his preparations. First, he bolted the door. Next, he extracted a magical candle from his pouch, lit it, and set it on the table. Then, he stretched out on the bed and closed his eyes.

Most magic folk were better at this than him. His mother could do it in a few blinks without anyone being the wiser, though when she really wanted a deep draught of knowledge, she settled in her chair beside the fire. His sister, Zoraida, powerful enchantress though she was, could not touch the vast store of ancestral magic memory that dwelt in her blood. It irritated her no end that a weak enchanter like him could access the knowledge he could barely use.

He'd tried to explain it to her, that it was much the same as dipping into his magic pouch and willing what he wanted to appear in his hand, but Zoraida would have none of it.

Which was probably why she fought dragons and he was here in this tiny mountain town, chasing visions and rumours and hoping he could save them. But tonight, he sought memories – memories of plagues past, how they started and how they were stopped.

He took a deep breath and let the memories flow.

Rats. Fleas. Floods. People dressed in clothing the like of which he'd never seen before. Likely long dead. Boils. Coughing. Something small enough to swim through the blood, like magic itself, but nowhere near as benign. And the dead, still carrying the sickness so even the gravediggers were not safe. Bodies were best burned.

Hours passed, or maybe it was just minutes. Millennia of memories marched past his eyes, the sights seen by thousands of magic users.

Yet when Zoticus surfaced, he knew one thing for certain: there was no cure for the plague. No herb or potion could touch it. A powerful healing spell might help, but healing was a power granted to few, and the touch of a spell so strong would leave its mark on the patient forever.

So, he could not cure it. But he could stop it from spreading, if he could banish every rat and flea from the town.

A Herculean task, if ever there was one.

But for an assassin who'd slain four heavily armed knights before their own armies, it would surely be a simple matter. The vermin stood no chance against him, and nor would the rats and fleas, either.

Fifteen

Silvana brought the wagon, piled high with sacks, a grim look on her face.

"Where is your father?" Sara asked.

"Probably in the inn, asleep on the floor. He's barely been home for days. If I didn't know how to work the mill, none of this would be ground." Silvana sighed. "I keep hoping he'll wake up and see there is still a world without Mother in it, but I'm not sure he even cares about me any more."

"He cares. I'm sure he cares. He just loved your mother so much…" Sara pulled the girl into a hug.

They stood there for what felt like a long time, yet Sara felt no need to break the embrace before Silvana was ready.

Eventually, Silvana pulled away, ducking her head as she sniffled. "I'm sorry. I just miss her so much, and he…"

Sara smiled awkwardly. "I lost my parents within days of one another, when I was not much older than you. My brothers, too. I know it isn't easy, but it's not easy for your father, either. When my husband died…I swear part of me died with him. If I hadn't had Tobias to care for, I might have lost myself in grief, too. Women are stronger than men will ever be, I fear. Not because we want to be, but because we must be. Without us, the world will fall apart. So we shed a few tears when it all becomes too much, but we go back to work when men would rather drink their way to the bottom of a barrel."

"That's not what the stories say. They're full of big, strong heroes who save helpless maidens from monsters," Silvana grumbled.

Sara laughed. "Of course they are. We all

have our fantasies, do we not? Women wish men were stronger, and more capable, so they won't need to do everything themselves, and men dream of being in charge, having women begging for their help instead of calling them fools for their latest blunder. Most men would not last a week without a woman to tell him what to do, and see that he has food."

"You're putting me off ever wanting to get married, then."

"Well, there are benefits of having a man around. They tend to chop the wood for you, and carry heavy things, and do some of the work around the farm…" Sara winked. "And in bed at night, a good husband is never too tired to make his wife happy."

Silvana's eyes grew wide with horror. "But that means babies! Noisy, helpless things that need more care than grown men!"

"But babies only happen once every nine months, and usually longer than that. Besides, you may change your mind when you hold your own child in your arms."

"Maybe." Silvana eyed the cart. "Do you want me to unload these?"

Sara considered, then shook her head. "No, let's put the cart away in the barn, and I'll find some labourers to do the heavy lifting. A day or two will not harm the flour – it'll be sitting in the cellar for months."

It took two of them to get the ponies to pull the cart into the barn, before turning them loose in Sara's field to snack on the stubble left over from the summer haymaking.

"Come inside for a cup of cider. I keep it cool in the cellar," Sara said, leading the way into the house while Silvana followed.

"What is that awful noise?" Silvana asked.

Deep in the cellar, Sara could not hear anything. She ascended the steps, listening hard.

Finally, Sara said, "It sounds like the time when Tobias found my grandfather's flute, and tried to play it like the travelling minstrels he'd seen in the town square. Terrible screeching. When he was asleep that night, I made sure to hide the flute where he might never find it again. But he should still be up in the high pasture…"

Now it was her turn to follow Silvana, out

the front door and down the road into town. A crowd of townspeople lined the roadside, transfixed by the bizarre parade headed their way.

The screeching music did indeed come from a flute, played by a figure in a brightly striped cloak that flew about him as he twirled and capered down the road. Behind him, a river of brown, black and white, followed.

Those by the roadside recoiled as the piper passed, pressing their backs to walls and fences in an effort to get away from him, though they could not stop staring.

At first, Sara thought it was the music that repelled them, until the river came close enough for Silvana to see what formed the flow.

"It's rats! A whole plague of rats! Thousands of them, following him!" she said. They horrified her even more than babies, judging by her expression.

The piper drew even with Sara, and he stopped to offer her a courtly bow.

"Master Zoticus!" she exclaimed. "What in heaven's name are you doing with all those rats?"

He straightened and grinned at her. "Why, saving your town from pestilence, my lady. Ridding it of all the rats." Another bow, and he resumed playing the flute.

There was a tune to it, of sorts, but it wasn't something one would want to dance to. Master Zoticus was no minstrel, that was for sure. He was a ratcatcher.

"Your pied piper is mad," said a new voice.

Ahab, of course. This time, Sara was inclined to agree with him. She'd never seen a man charm rats before. Why would anyone want to?

Yet Zoticus seemed too sure of himself to be mad.

Little though she liked rats, she wanted to follow him to see where he took them.

No, that would be foolish. She'd have a better view from her worktable behind the house. And she'd avoid the rats.

She watched Zoticus take his river of rats down to the lake, where he boarded a boat — with Matteo at the oars, no less — and headed out over the water.

The rats followed him blindly, jumping off the dock and into the lake. They swam for a bit, until they went under, and did not surface. Hundreds of them at a time.

Sara shuddered. There had to be twoscore rats for every man, woman and child in Mirroten. Had there really been so many? Or had Zoticus brought them here?

When all the rats had disappeared, Matteo turned the boat around, and Zoticus took an oar to help the old man row back to shore. He'd thrown his striped cloak off, and Sara couldn't help but stare as the muscles in his arms rippled at every stroke.

He was well-fed for a ratcatcher, and likely as strong as any man in Mirroten. He stepped from the boat to the dock with the grace of a practiced sailor, too.

And then he shaded his eyes from the sun, and peered up the hill, to where she stood staring. He directed another deep bow in her direction, and Sara felt her cheeks redden.

"Now there's a man who thinks a lot of himself," Tola said.

Sara started. She'd been so busy watching

Zoticus she hadn't even noticed her friend's arrival.

"I bet he's terrible in bed," Tola added.

Sara sighed. Such men usually were. "But it doesn't hurt to dream," she said.

"He'll have half the girls in town dreaming about him tonight, not just you."

Sara shrugged. "As long as I have him to myself in the dream, they may do what they like."

"There's magic about him, Swanhild said. He's still susceptible to her spell, but I think he knew she'd cast it. She said he came looking for me, at first, but it seems he found you and liked you better. He hasn't said a word to me."

There was a strange twisting sensation in Sara's belly, and she wasn't sure if it was good or bad. "Have you come to warn me to be careful?"

Tola snorted. "He didn't set off my door enchantment, and Swanhild said he was well-spoken and polite. I don't believe he means harm to anyone in Mirroten. Maybe I'm wrong, and he'd be delightful in bed. Most men with magic in their blood learn to respect the women in their family, for it must run strong in the female line for it to show up in the boys. Swanhild did say he asked for directions. Most unusual in a man."

"So you think I should seduce him?" Sara asked.

"Oh no. I think you should consider allowing him to seduce you. And if you do allow him to share your bed, promise to tell me about it."

They both laughed, but they also watched Zoticus stride up the road back into town.

Sara wet her lips. Perhaps she would.

Sixteen

Zoticus might not be able to read minds, but he'd known what the woman from his vision was thinking while she watched him today. And while his vision of her wasn't about to happen today, he was pretty sure he knew he'd see her again soon – that very evening, if he wasn't mistaken.

He told himself the rats and fleas were the reason he'd bathed and changed into clean clothes, while leaving today's things to be laundered by the inn's maid. He debated whether to go down to the taproom for dinner, where she might easily find him, but she seemed the sort of lady who would wish to see him privately, and the inn staff would honour her wishes.

So he ate dinner alone in his room, then stretched out on the bed. Whether she arrived early or late, she'd probably appreciate it if he was well-rested for whatever she had in mind. And he'd enjoy it more if he wasn't tired.

He slipped easily into dreams of her, and was woken by a tap at the door.

"Yes?" he said.

"There's someone to see you, Master Zoticus," the maid said. There was a quaver in her voice that hadn't been there before.

It would not do to greet her from his bed. Too presumptuous. He hadn't bothered to undress, so it took him a moment to pull on some boots before he answered, "You can come in." He placed himself by the table, where he'd left a jug of wine and two cups. The inn's best wine, he'd been told, and he'd tasted enough to know it was at least drinkable.

Then the door creaked open, and two men crowded inside. Rough labourers, by the look of them, used to hard work and heavy lifting. Men who could not afford an assassin and who would never be targeted by one, because commoners like them were not above the law, especially when noblemen were the ones who enforced it.

But they were smart enough to fear him.

"Master Zoticus, you are summoned to a meeting at the town hall," one of them said.

"By whom?"

By all that was holy, he wanted to know the name of the woman in his vision. Then again, if she was the sort to summon him to her bed, he wasn't sure if she was worth the trouble.

The two men eyed each other nervously, as if daring the other man to say her name first.

Finally, the one who'd already spoken said, "By Elder Ahab, head of the town council."

Zoticus did his best to hide his surprise. The head of the council had seemed more like a useless puffer fish than any real kind of authority, but this man wasn't lying. So either this Ahab had summoned him, or the woman had told these two the summons was at Ahab's order, and they'd believed her.

He relaxed. Yes, that seemed more likely.

Zoticus swept a light cloak about his shoulders. "What are we waiting for, then? To the town hall we must go!"

The men breathed twin sighs of relief as they accompanied him out of the inn.

Zoticus glimpsed the maid's wide eyes watching from a darkened doorway before she hid her face. Why did they all fear him, when this morning they hadn't cared about how much they stared at him? It couldn't have been the rats, or his skill with the high-pitched enchanted flute his mother had given him. The instrument's shrill whistle was enough to melt earwax, even before she'd enchanted it to summon any creature he cared to name.

Idly, he wondered if it would work on dragons.

Zoticus shook his head. Something to consider later, when he had someone more experienced in fighting dragons by his side.

To his surprise, the sun was already peeping over the horizon. He'd slept longer than he'd thought. Why the lady would want to see him so early in the day…ah, but this was a farming town, not a trading city like Rialto. Days went from dawn until dusk in places like this, and perhaps she'd fallen into the same pattern.

Zoticus stepped into the town hall, where a lone candle cast more shadows than light.

"Bring him here."

The voice did not belong to a woman.

Zoticus peered into the darkness, waiting for his eyes to adjust. Ah, there was the man who'd spoken.

Ahab sat just outside the candle's pool of light, with a cup in one hand and a jug by his elbow. Judging by his sloppy movements, he'd been drinking a while. Most of the night, if Zoticus was any judge.

"You. Assassin. You brought this evil to my town," he slurred.

For a moment, it felt like someone's cold hand squeezed his heart inside his chest.

But Zoticus's head was quicker than his heart.

He couldn't have brought the plague here. Every rat and flea in the town now lay dead and drowned at the bottom of the lake. He'd arrived in town with only the contents of his magical pouch, and nothing he placed in that pouch survived the enchantment. He'd left a piece of ham in the pocket of his summer cloak when he'd stashed it away, and pulled the same piece out, more than a year later, as fresh as the day it had been sliced.

But this wasn't about ham. It wasn't about him, either.

"What evil might that be?" Zoticus asked.

"Your evil. We're good people. We work hard, go to church, pray and live virtuous lives, but you! You kill for money. Is it not written in God's commandments that we must not kill?"

"And it also says in the Bible that men shouldn't wear both linen and wool, and women shouldn't cook meat with milk," Zoticus replied. He'd read the entire tome, had an illuminated copy in his pouch somewhere, actually, and it made his ancestral memories seem positively orderly in comparison. Not that he'd say that to the pope who'd given him the enormous book. "And the whole book is full of people killing each other, for all manner of crimes, not just mixing linen and wool, or meat and milk."

"Do not lie to me! Are you not Master Zoticus the assassin, who has slayed countless men the world over, enough to fill a river with their blood?" Ahab demanded.

"I am Master Zoticus, and I keep count," Zoticus snapped. "Of the men I have killed, and of their victims. A river? If they had lived, they could have filled an ocean with the blood and tears of their victims, and the families who mourn them, but those victims and their families have justice now because of me!"

"And what of my daughter? Why did you kill her? What crime can sweet Ysabel have committed, that you saw fit to kill her? How much did they pay you?" Ahab's eyes were wild now, with a madness Zoticus recognised, though too late. A grieving father would do anything to revenge a favourite child.

Zoticus shook his head, lifting his hands up in surrender. "I never met your daughter. I cannot have killed her. You are mistaken. Someone else must have done this terrible deed. Perhaps I can help you…"

Ahab pointed a shaking finger at him. "You have done enough. It was you, and no one else, with your evil, that has brought this plague upon us! Upon her, the sweetest girl who ever lived..."

Horror seized Zoticus's tongue, rendering him speechless. Even if he could have spoken, he had no words. He was wrong. The plague had touched this town, and he was too late to save them. He had to warn the woman in his vision...

He turned to leave, but a glancing blow struck his head, and everything went white for a moment. A second blow turned it all black.

Seventeen

Sara found her mind drifting in church that morning. Perhaps it was because Zoticus had been in her dreams so much the night before, she'd woken several times, convinced he was in her bedchamber. Of course he hadn't been, but getting back to sleep hadn't been easy.

Or perhaps it was because Father Fazzio kept droning on and on about how they had to reject evil and protect their virtue, as he'd been doing every day since they'd heard about the plague in Altino. It made her wonder if Fazzio thought the town was a flock of white-clad virgins, the sort who'd never done anything in their lives, let alone commit a single sin.

She suppressed a snort. No one in the town over the age of three could possibly be without sin. And there was the whole concept of original sin, that they'd all inherited from Adam and Eve, or so Father Fazzio had told them back in May, when some of the teenagers in town had tried to celebrate some pagan fertility rite. Actually, she remembered trying something similar with Tobias's father when they'd been that age. Of course, they'd gone up to the high pasture instead of into the forest, so no one had interrupted their private celebration. One they'd repeated every year until Tobias was born. Come to think of it, Tobias might have been conceived up there in the high pasture…perhaps the old fertility rites still had power.

"And we will be conducting a prayer vigil for Ysabel this evening. All are invited to attend," Fazzio finished.

Wait…Ysabel?

When the mass ended, she kept her eyes on Ahab, hoping to catch him before he left. He hurried out of the church, and she could barely keep him in sight as he strode off toward the town green. He reached the door of his cottage, and for a moment, he hesitated with his hand on the door handle.

"Ahab, is Ysabel…is she all right?" Sara called as she approached.

Ahab slowly turned to face her, and he didn't need to open his mouth to answer her.

She pressed her hand to her mouth. "Oh, no. How bad is she? Is there anything I can do?"

A harsh laugh came out of his throat, unlike any noise she'd ever heard him make before. "Oh, you've already done enough. Instead of driving the evil out of town, like any sensible person should have, you let him stay. And he killed her. That vile wretch killed my Ysabel!"

His words made no sense. "Someone killed Ysabel? You mean…she wasn't ill?"

"Before he came, she was fine. She filled all the mattresses on her own – she insisted upon it. But the night he came, she fell ill. Deathly ill. So suddenly it seemed like a curse, something only the most evil wretch could have possibly cast upon her. He had all of the town fawning over him, watching that spectacle yesterday, while his curse stole her life away. That assassin killed my daughter, and I will have justice!"

"Ahab…" she began. The death of his daughter had evidently driven the man mad. "What assassin?"

"Your pied piper, the capering fool I saw you making sheep's eyes at yesterday," Ahab spat. "The man you allowed into our town, who you welcomed into your service…is none other than Master Assassin Zoticus, a demon who has slain more men than the very devil himself. The bishop himself sent warning to Father Fazzio only yesterday that the assassin might be headed our way, and should he arrive here, we should send him straight to the bishop to face justice for his crimes. Alas, the warning arrived too late for Ysabel."

It beggared belief. "But why would anyone want Ysabel dead?" She was perhaps the only person in town who might have fitted Father Fazzio's image of an innocent virgin, for heaven knew the girl had rarely been well enough to spend time with boys her own age.

"You'd have to ask that demon…that wolf in sheep's clothing…but I beg you, do not. Stay away from him, lest he kill you, too. He's already charmed you, like the devil he is, and with his every breath, he expels more pestilence. Save yourself, and stay away. I've had him locked away, where he cannot harm anyone else in the town, and I will send someone to fetch some of the bishop's men, for it will take a heavy guard to escort a demon to Rialto."

Amid all the madness, one thing became clear.

"Ysabel died of the plague? The plague has come to Mirroten?" Sara asked. She didn't want to believe it.

"Carried by that demon of an assassin, Master Zoticus himself!" Ahab yanked open his door, strode into his cottage, then slammed the door in her face.

If the plague had indeed come to Mirroten…

"Heaven help us all," Sara whispered.

Eighteen

Zoticus woke to the sound of something grinding above him. That placed him…in the cellar beneath the mill, most likely. He reached for the back of his head, and found his hair sticky with dried blood, but his healing amulet had taken care of the wound and the headache he probably would have woken with, without magical assistance. He'd worn the amulet around his neck since leaving Rialto – one couldn't be too careful with plague about.

Enough daylight reached the cellar that he knew it was likely the middle of the day outside, and not a good time to escape, if he didn't want to be seen. The town would see enough death with the plague — they didn't need anyone dying at his hands when he escaped. It was best for everybody if he waited until night.

In the meantime, he was at leisure to explore his cell. They'd laid him on a well-stuffed straw pallet, with a blanket that could have been the twin of the one he'd slept under in the inn. A jug of water sat on the floor beside him, along with a basket of food that would feed a family for an entire day. Bread, cheese, apples, and a chunk of meat he suspected had come from a goat.

Drink first, then something to eat. He uncorked the jug and breathed deeply. That definitely wasn't water. Strong cider, if he wasn't mistaken. He wasn't sure if his jailers wanted him drunk and easier to deal with, or whether this was normal prisoner fare for Mirroten. If they treated prisoners so well, it was a surprise they didn't have more of them.

Perhaps he should stay for a few days, until the plague ended their hospitality. He could do with a rest, and the cider would certainly help him with that.

But he still had to warn the woman in his vision.

Zoticus sighed. Tonight, then. After he'd demolished the dinner they'd provided.

Nineteen

It felt surreal returning to the church that evening for Ysabel's vigil. The whole town was there, heads bowed in grief for a girl none of them would have said was deserving of death.

"Did you hear about the assassin?"

Sara lifted her head to find Silvana at her elbow. "I heard something, yes." A little from Ahab, more from Fazzio, and a great deal from Tola, for the man had quite the reputation in Rialto.

"Elder Ahab had him locked in Father's cellar. He means to keep him there for some days. Elder Ahab said he killed Ysabel. Is it true?"

Sara lowered her voice. "Elder Ahab is mad with grief. He is likely to say many things, both true and untrue. I myself have heard him say Master Zoticus killed Ysabel, yet in the next breath he swore she died of the plague. I'm not sure what I fear most – whether Ahab has accused an innocent man of murder, or whether he has imprisoned an assassin so deadly, he will surely exact vengeance on the whole town. Even if he is an assassin…why Ysabel? If someone wanted these lands so badly, surely their assassin would choose a more suitable target…" Her voice died.

Tobias. If anyone wanted her family's lands, they'd have to kill Tobias.

She had to know.

"Go…go in without me. I'll catch up," Sara said, gesturing for Silvana to enter the candle-lit church. The summer night seemed colder than it should, but she let the darkness cloak her as she hurried away.

If she wanted to speak to Zoticus alone, now would be the best time, with everyone at the church. To ask him if he really was an assassin, and whether Tobias was in danger.

And, if so…to do whatever it took to save Tobias.

Because Ahab had loved Ysabel, but it was nothing compared to the fierce love Sara harboured for her only son. As long as she drew breath, she would do everything within her power to save him. From assassins, from the plague…and anything else that threatened him.

Heaven help the man who stood in her way.

She marched down to the silent mill. The cellar had a set of double doors, wide enough to allow a wagon inside, barred with an enormous beam that usually took two men to lift.

Yet when she raised her lantern high to look for something that might allow her to lever it open, she found the beam on the floor, and the doors open wide.

Inside the cellar itself was an empty pallet, and no sign of the man except for the faint outline where he'd lay before he'd left.

Sara snorted softly. It seemed heaven had

already helped Master Zoticus. Heaven, or the devil.

Whoever had helped him, it mattered not. He had to be headed out of town, and there was only one road. If she followed it, she'd soon catch up to him.

He wouldn't escape her so easily.

Twenty

Finally, the sun called it a day. Zoticus stretched, pocketed the last of the bread and cheese, and dug out his lock-picking charm. All right, it was actually a key, but he had yet to find the lock it had been made for. The enchantment allowed it to work without being inserted into a lock, though he did still have to pay a blood price, like with any magic.

Tonight, the door seemed to be particularly stubborn. A drop or two of blood was usually enough, but this time, it wasn't until the key was coated in his blood and threatening to slip out of his fingers that the doors finally opened.

The people of Mirroten really wanted him to stay, didn't they?

He stepped over the beam that had once barred the doors and headed up to the road. No one was about, though there were lights further up the hill, around the church.

Some local saint's day, perhaps, or some other holy day he'd forgotten. He wasn't even sure what day it was any more, let alone the date. The church would have to forgive his absence. The people of Mirroten certainly wouldn't welcome him.

So he followed the road the other way — away from the town. Lake water lapped softly at the dock, reminding him he could borrow a boat and follow the river all the way to the Rialto lagoon. The boat's owner would likely be dead of plague within weeks, so he wouldn't even miss it.

Tempting, but his instincts told him no. Instead, he stayed on the road, just long enough to be well away from Mirroten, before he set up camp.

As the town fell behind him so only

moonlight lit his way, Zoticus became aware of a second set of footsteps following him.

He paused. When the footsteps continued, he ghosted into the trees. Godfrey had never understood this was why Zoticus always wore grey. A man didn't need magic to become invisible.

Soon enough, a figure approached. A lantern hanging from their hand illuminated the road around the figure's boots, and little more.

Now it was Zoticus's turn to do the following, but his footfalls were silent and swift. The first the figure knew of his presence was the knife he pressed to her throat.

For with his free arm around her body, he was left in no doubt that she was a woman.

One who was too scared to scream or struggle.

"Why are you following me?" he hissed in her ear.

"First, to find out if you really are an assassin, but I suppose I already have my answer to that," she said.

The woman from his vision.

Her heart beat fast beneath his hand, but there was no fear in her tone.

He relaxed, but didn't yet lower the blade.

"The second was to return your things, which you left in the inn."

Zoticus cursed inwardly. He wasn't normally this careless, but he could afford to replace all of the commonplace items he'd left in the inn.

"And third, I have a commission I wish you to undertake."

Every word was the truth.

He released her and tucked his knife back into his belt. "I choose which commissions I take."

"So I have heard. You don't kill anyone except those you are commissioned to kill, and even then, no one is entirely sure you are responsible. Even Holy Crusaders, at the head of an army."

She had a source of information who was unusually well informed. Better than Ahab or the other townsfolk. If he had to guess, he'd pick, "Mistress Tola, the witch from Rialto?"

"Yes. How did Ysabel die?"

His throat grew tight. "I wasn't there, so I

don't know. Her father said it was the plague. If the man was correct..." He didn't have the heart to tell her that everyone she knew would die.

Ah, but she already knew. "If the plague has come to Mirroten, then my people will suffer the same fate as everyone in Altino." Her shoulders slumped.

"Not everyone. I survived." The moment the words left his lips, he regretted them. No matter what the monks said, he could not work miracles, and that's what it would take to save Mirroten if ridding it of rats and fleas was not enough.

"How?"

"Magic, and luck. Luck that I survived the plague once before, coming home from a crusade. And magic...magic which won't work on anyone but me." He set off down the road again, not caring if she followed.

Of course, she did.

"Where are you going?" she called.

"To make camp far enough away from your town so I can sleep."

"I know the best spots for travellers to

camp between towns. I'll show you."

He could probably find them on his own, but he did not refuse her offer. Something told him he needed to hear more about the job she wished to offer him.

He let the silence swell between them, wondering if she would break it with chatter. Most people could not abide silence for long.

This lady was not most people.

He smiled in the dark.

"What's funny?" she asked.

A thought came to him, and he ran with it. "What would your husband say, if he could see you now, following some assassin you barely know down the road, away from your home?"

He expected her to stop and blush, or come to her senses and turn back.

Instead, her voice was cold as her steps never slowed. "It might surprise you to learn that the lands of Mirroten are quite extensive, so in truth, I have not yet left home. Besides, I imagine my husband is far too busy doing important things, instead of watching what's going on down here. But if he were watching over me, I imagine he'd approve of my willingness to do what I must for those I care about."

Now he was the one who hung his head in shame. "You are a widow. I'm sorry for your loss." He refused to focus on the spark of hope that leaped into life at the thought of her having no husband.

"As am I, but I still have my son. He'll be a man soon, old enough to claim his birthright."

There was a bitter note in her voice, but it seemed that the bitterness was directed at him, not the son.

"There's the camp I use when I trade with the other towns." She lifted her lantern and pointed.

The clearing held little more than a fire pit ringed around with stones, and a small pile of firewood left by some kindly traveller.

Or the lady herself?

No, surely one of her servants.

She made no effort to help him as he set up some kindling and set it alight. Soon, he had a small fire going.

Without rising from his knees, he held out his hand to the still standing woman. "My things, please?"

Wordlessly, she handed him his travelling sack, which felt heavier than he remembered it.

Perhaps because she'd packed his freshly laundered clothes, a flagon of wine and other provisions. Mirroten might not be the friendliest town, but at least they were generous with their hospitality.

The least he could do was share what little hospitality he had here. He spread the striped cloak on the ground for her, and set the wine flagon between them.

"Now, please sit, my lady, and tell me about this commission you have in mind."

She set the lantern down beside the cloak. "Sara."

Her name! His lady finally had a name! He couldn't remember the last time he'd felt this jubilant. "If it please my Lady Sara, will you sit and share a cup of wine with me while you tell me what you desire?"

He didn't mean it to come out so seductive. He just…she…

She laughed. She laughed so hard she fell to her knees and rolled onto her side on the striped cloak. "It's Sara. Just Sara. And Tola was right!"

No, he would not fall into this trap. There was a reason few assassins lived as long as he had.

"You live in the grandest house in Mirroten, and the town and all the land surrounding it belongs to your family, does it not?"

She nodded once.

"So much land would not be granted to anyone less than a knight. So, your husband…"

She laughed harder. "My husband was a goatherder, and a good man. He had a silver tongue and a sweet smile, but he never held a sword in his life, nor did he need to."

So the land was hers. "What of your father?"

She sobered. "My father was a good man. He took his place on the town council, and he was so busy running the estate he had no time for swordplay or horses that weren't for working. My brothers, had they lived…some of them hoped to be trained as knights. Much like my grandfather, and his father, whose swords are still mounted on a wall in the house somewhere. I think it was my great grandfather who was a crusader knight. The king gave him the estate to honour his service in the Holy Land."

That must have been the very first crusade — a more honourable affair than the one Zoticus had joined. Though he'd seen tavern brawls more honourable, if truth be told, so that wasn't saying much.

"Which would make him a baron, and you…Lady Sara, liege lord to everyone who lives here."

Slowly, she shook her head. "No. Their liege lord will be Tobias, my son." She lifted her gaze to meet his eyes. "Enough banter. From what I have seen and what I have heard, you are a man of honour and honesty. If I ask you a question, will you tell me the truth?"

"I will not lie."

She inclined her head. "That is fair. Now, tell me — did you come to Mirroten to kill my son?"

Why would she think that? Had someone threatened her in the past? Surely they'd have wanted both her and the son dead, for the lands were hers.

She mistook his silence for something else. "If you have come to kill him, I will pay you double to stay your hand."

He should have told her the truth instantly, instead of weighing her words. Now he'd sound like he was lying.

"Triple."

What could he say? Triple of nothing was still nothing. He didn't kill children.

She leaned forward, her eyes glittering in the firelight. "Name your price. If it is within my power to grant it to you, I will give you whatever you want, if you will swear to save my son."

All he wanted right now was her.

Perhaps it was the cider he'd been drinking all day, or some intoxicating scent she wore, or the spell she wove with words alone…he no longer cared why.

He kissed her.

Twenty-One

May God forgive her, but once his lips touched hers, Sara forgot she'd ever had a son. She was aware of nothing but that moment. The tart taste of cider on his tongue, his warm breath mingling with hers, his fingers tracing her jaw as one kiss became all the seduction she could ever need to succumb.

Until it stopped.

Zoticus froze, and it was like kissing a corpse. Farewelling a love she'd known but briefly, which would never be enough.

She moved away from him, putting a more

decorous distance between them. For a moment, she'd been willing to give him all of herself, but he'd declined. Good. One of them should be sensible when business dealings and lives hung in the balance.

Finally, he moved. "The castle in the mountains," he said, or something like it, before shaking his head.

"It's not a castle. It's a monastery. The Cloister of the Holy Innocents, built by the king to house the relics my ancestor brought back from his crusade. The remains of the Holy Innocents," Sara said.

Zoticus drew in a sharp breath. "Have you been there?"

She let out a laugh. "In case you haven't noticed, I'm a woman. Women aren't welcome in monasteries. Apparently we distract the men from their work."

"Men who are easily distracted must not be very good at their jobs."

Unlike him.

She sighed. "Perhaps. I don't imagine I'd be much of a distraction now. Perhaps they might allow me to visit."

"But first you wish me to save your son."

She eyed him across the fire. "First, I wish to hear you swear you will not kill my son. Then, I want you to save him. If someone sent you to kill him, what will stop them from sending another?" She reached for the pouch at her belt, untied it, and tossed the pouch into his lap.

He lifted it, shaking it so the coins inside tinkled sweetly. "What is this for?"

"That is for ridding us of rats. I have no desire to be indebted to you. Now, what will it cost me for you to save my son?"

He gazed at her through the flames. He looked so long, she feared he was reading her soul. Finally, he said, "Lady Sara, the only payment I ask is the honour of serving you."

She wanted to believe him. Truly, she did. But he was an assassin, sent to kill her son. Though he talked of honour, she still didn't know what that meant to an assassin. Perhaps he had honour.

Or maybe he had none.

She wrapped the striped cloak around her and leaned back against the tree behind her.

"Then we should get some sleep, so that on the morrow we can head back to Mirroten for my son."

"You would sleep alone in the forest with an assassin you barely know? You're braver than most men I have known, Lady Sara."

Better than sharing his bed, she thought to herself as she felt her face heat. Now that would be foolish.

"No, Master Zoticus. I intend to spend the night keeping watch while you sleep, so that you do not sneak away. We have a bargain, you and I. You desire honour, and I want you to save my son. Come morning, I intend to see both our wishes granted."

"If you truly knew my wishes and desires, you would hurry back to your own bed in Mirroten tonight, my lady."

His words made her spine shiver, but she refused to let him see the effect he had on her. He was handsome enough to consider making him her lover, but she'd be the one to bury a blade in his breast if he so much as shed a drop of Tobias's blood.

"You're on my family's land, assassin.

Whether we are in Mirroten or in the monastery on the mountain or here in my camp, my power is the same." Even she heard the cold, naked threat in her voice – a tone she'd never used before. She suspected even Ahab would quail if he'd heard it.

Zoticus, the wretch, merely grinned. "Lady Sara, I suspect your power is greater than you know. I am, of course, yours to command. Sleep, you say? Then I shall."

He stretched out, rolling himself up in his own cloak, before resting his head on his sack of belongings. Within moments, he began to snore.

Twenty-Two

Sunlight filtering through the trees woke Zoticus, who had to admit he'd slept quite well. So had Lady Sara, it seemed, who had fallen asleep to the sound of his fake snoring. She was fortunate that he had magical means of keeping watch, that didn't rely on her ability to stay awake. Not that he'd expected to be attacked – there were too few people left alive to do so, after the plague had passed through. And he'd hear an angry mob from Mirroten a mile away – more than enough time to awaken and hide.

He broke his bread in half and used his knife to spread the remaining cheese across both pieces. "Would you like to break your fast, Lady Sara?"

Her eyes flew open and for a moment they stared at him in shock. Then she recovered, sat up, and said, "Yes, thank you, Master Zoticus." She accepted the offered bread and cheese.

Even brave Melisende had suspected poison the first time he'd handed her food. Yet Lady Sara bit into her breakfast without hesitation.

"Aren't you worried I'll poison you?" he asked.

She shrugged. "If you poison me, you won't be paid. You may speak of honour, but a man who kills for a living expects to be paid. An assassin with your reputation would not have lived this long if he were a fool, and nothing I have seen so far has made me think otherwise, even if you do own a motley cloak."

He felt his cheeks redden. "It was a gift from a friend."

She rose, dusted off the cloak she'd slept in, and held it out to him. "Then I should return it. My thanks for loaning me such a precious gift."

He wasn't sure if she was simply being courteous, or trying to taunt him. "If ever you have need of my cloak again, you have only to ask, my lady."

Her fiery eyes said hell would freeze over before she'd ask any such thing. But she finished her breakfast, then washed her hands daintily with a flask of water.

"I'm ready to leave as soon as you are," she said.

It wasn't long before they were headed back along the road to Mirroten. Somehow he'd ended up carrying his things and her lantern, so she had both hands free to pick berries from the bushes beside the road as they walked.

The first person who spotted them was a girl with flour-dusted skirts.

Zoticus glanced at Sara, wondering if she'd want him to hide so that she might pretend that she hadn't seen him, but she was too busy greeting the girl.

"Mistress Sara, you must do something. Ahab has everyone locked in the church, and he won't let Father Fazzio release them until they agree to go on a crusade!"

"Ahab has the whole town locked in the church?" Zoticus swore. If even one of them was afflicted with the plague, they might pass the pestilence on to everyone. Better to burn the church down than release them, if they were all going to die anyway. Not to mention suffocating from smoke inhalation was a far more merciful way to die than succumbing to the plague.

The girl shook her head. "No, not the whole town. Just the children, and anyone who isn't married yet."

"Tobias?" Sara asked.

"Yes, him too."

For a moment, Sara looked stricken. But only for a moment.

Her hand landed on his arm. "Master Zoticus, you will free the children from the church. Take them to the travelling camp, where I will meet you with supplies for the journey."

What? What had he missed that suddenly he had to steal an entire town's children? They weren't rats, responding to a magic whistle. And there was absolutely no way he was taking children on a crusade. He wouldn't have even taken Melisende if he hadn't seen that vision where she helped him get justice from those damned knights.

"I'm not taking kids on a crusade!" he burst out.

Her hand on his arm squeezed gently. "Bring them to the travelling camp, and I will explain everything," Sara said. Then she grew thoughtful. "Goats. We'll need to bring the goats." She hurried off, beckoning for the miller girl to follow her.

Too late, Zoticus realised he'd somehow gone from saving one boy to kidnapping half the town. If it had been anyone else asking, he would have chased after them to argue, but instinct told him he'd be wasting his time today.

Lady Sara was certainly a force to be reckoned with.

He wagered she'd be wondrous in bed. A pity his vision had cut short last night's kiss, or he might already know.

At least if they were to journey together, they might have another chance.

Then again, maybe not with a hundred children coming along.

He sighed. He'd find a way. Eventually.

Or she would…

Twenty-Three

The people of Mirroten liked putting bloody big bars across their doors, Zoticus decided, struggling to unbar the church door. He'd pull out his magic key to do the job if he had to, but he shouldn't have to. It was simply a matter of the right leverage and…finally. He leaned the bar against the wall and threw open the church doors.

The town's children, huddled at the other end of the church, before the altar, squinted in the sunlight streaming into the windowless building. Two of the bigger boys, old enough to consider young men, stood before the group, ready to defend them.

Zoticus had to admire their courage.

The smaller of the two stepped forward. "You may tell Elder Ahab that our vigil has not changed our resolve. We will not go with you on a crusade to the Holy Land."

Zoticus did not remember madness being one of the early symptoms of plague, but it did seem like absurd ideas were spreading faster than usual through the town.

"Good," Zoticus replied. "Because one crusade is more than enough for any man. I'll not be going on another. Anyone with any sense will not be heading for the Holy Land, but in the opposite direction. Up into the mountains, maybe, until the plague has passed."

The boy frowned. "You mean on a pilgrimage, to see some holy relics?"

Yes. Some remote place with holy relics, high in the mountains. Somewhere so hard to get to, the plague had not reached it yet.

"You mean like the Cloister of the Holy Innocents? To see the jewel encrusted skeletons?" the bigger boy blurted out.

The smaller boy turned to him. "You've been there?"

He shrugged. "Master Gojko journeys there once a year to trade herbs. They have some rather unusual ones that only grow high in the mountains, and because the Rialto traders can't go any further up the river, he buys extra to take to the Cloister. I used to go with him when I was younger, but now he leaves me to tend the shop while he's gone."

The apothecary's apprentice, Zoticus presumed.

"Could you take us there?" Zoticus asked.

The boy shrugged. "Maybe. Once you're on the right road, it's hard to get lost. Why? Who's going to the monastery? It'll be autumn soon, and the high passes won't be open much longer. One decent snowfall and you're stuck there until spring."

That sounded perfect. "We all are, if we want to survive this plague."

The smaller boy was not as trusting as the apothecary's apprentice. "Why should we go anywhere with you? This is our town. We're not rats, to be driven out and drowned."

Zoticus winced. He hadn't expected this to go well, but this was worse than he'd expected. "Because Lady Sara told me to take you."

The two boys exchanged glances. The bigger one shook his head. "You take it up with her. I wouldn't dare argue with Mistress Sara."

The smaller one nodded. "I'd better get the goats. I'll never hear the end of it if I leave them behind."

Before Zoticus could stop him, the boy darted out of the church, toward the town green.

Zoticus stared after him. Should he go after him, or just save the rest of the children? Lady Sara had said to save all of them, but perhaps she hadn't considered him coming up against the obstinate goat boy.

"Do you think he'll come back?" Zoticus asked the apothecary's apprentice.

"Of course. Tobias said he was going to get the goats. It might take a while to get them all moving, but even he knows better than to cross his mum."

Zoticus's heart sank. Of course the boy was Sara's son.

"Take everyone here down the road to the first traveller's camp to wait for me. We'll meet you there, with or without the goats," Zoticus said. Without, if he had his way. Animals would only slow their progress up the mountain.

The boy nodded and started issuing orders to the rest of the children.

Zoticus headed for the town green. Saving Sara's son was proving harder than he'd thought.

Twenty-Four

"I haven't even managed to get the cart unloaded," Sara admitted as she opened the barn. "Probably a good thing, as now we have less to load. Wherever we'll go, we'll need supplies. It could be months before it's safe to come back."

"Where will we go?" Silvana asked.

Sara sank onto a bench, burying her head in her hands. "I don't know." When she'd asked Zoticus to save Tobias, she'd meant for the two of them to travel someplace far away, where they'd be safe from the plague. Two people could easily disappear, with enough coin to pay for whatever they needed along the way. But half the town…

Even Sara did not have enough coin to pay to feed and house so many. They'd have to rely on the charity of strangers, a chancy thing in good times, but if the plague had truly wiped out the other towns along the river, who was left that they could turn to?

If Mercurio had not gone far, perhaps he could be persuaded to take everyone aboard his ship. If they were to travel aboard a ship, though, they'd need to take all their provisions with them. She'd need everything on the cart, and most of the contents of her cellar, too. Not to mention another cart, or creatures who could carry things. Mirroten did not have anywhere near enough ponies to take a tenth of what she had stored in the cellar…

"I'll get the goats," she said.

"No need, my lady. You have only to wish, and it shall appear."

"Master Zoticus?" Even Sara had to stare as the man appeared in the middle of a flock of what looked like the whole town's goats. She shook her head. Goats were difficult to handle at the best of times, or so Tobias and her husband had told her. How an assassin could get them to behave so well…it would take some powerful magic.

"Mother?" Tobias appeared, and the riddle was solved. "Master Zoticus here said we were to meet you at one of the travelling camps along the road, before heading up the mountain, but Raphael told me it takes some time to get there, and they are not accustomed to hosting guests. We'd do well to bring our own supplies. Now, the goats have only carried sacks of hay down from the high pasture in the past, but if we could keep their loads light, we might be able to take some of the sacks of chestnut flour…"

Between the four of them, they managed to load most of the cart's contents onto the goats, and fill the cart with casks from the cellar. Silvana brought a second cart, which was soon full, too. Sara set the pigs loose in the chestnut orchard, hoping she'd be able to return before they ate next year's harvest. Surely she wouldn't be gone that long.

"Did you see Mercurio's ship on your way to Mirroten, Master Zoticus? He could not have gone far. Perhaps if I rode ahead, I could catch him and ask him to return for the rest of us. With his new ship, he can surely take us anywhere we want. Far from the reach of this plague."

He stared at her for a moment, then muttered an oath. "Mercurio the river trader made it to your town? No wonder the plague came here, too – he was carrying it aboard his ship. Yes, I found the trader's ship, but his corpse was already cold. The plague took him, too. The ship was tainted, so I burned it."

Her heart sank. "Then where will we go?"

Tobias made an impatient sound. "Have you forgotten, Mother? Master Zoticus is taking us up to the monastery in the mountains."

She blinked. It made sense, now that she thought about it. What better place than a church dedicated to the Holy Innocents to shelter her town's children from this scourge? "Of course," she said. "Let me get a few things from the house, and we shall go."

By the time she returned with a sack of

clothes for herself and Tobias, she found only Zoticus waiting for her.

"Where is my son?" she asked.

He jerked his head toward the road. "He and the miller's girl went on ahead with the goats and one of the carts, leaving the other one for you. I said I'd wait for you."

For a moment, her heart softened toward him. It was a sweet gesture, waiting to make sure she wasn't left behind. Like something a friend would do.

But Zoticus was not her friend.

"So much for protecting my son. What if something happens to him while you were waiting for me?" Sara snapped.

Zoticus merely shrugged, as if her anger meant nothing to him. "He's got a hundred goats and the miller's girl, armed with a stout cudgel. If anyone had wanted to stop us from leaving, they've had ample chance, yet I've seen no one. The last time I saw a town this quiet, it was Altino, and it was because everyone was dead. I didn't want to say it in front of the children, who all seem to be in good health, but everyone who wasn't locked in that church might be infected, or already dead."

Sara sighed heavily. "Yes, I haven't seen anyone about, either. Can it…can this plague really strike people down so quickly? One day they seem in perfect health, and the next day, they are dead?"

"Once the infection takes hold, death comes quickly. Usually a few days, but sometimes less. It can hide in the body, not coming out to kill right away, waiting several days or even a week. It can spread through rats, fleas…and sometimes, between one person and another, through the very air we breathe."

"Creeping in the dark, where we cannot see, only to strike us down without warning…this disease sounds much like an assassin," she said.

Zoticus frowned. "There you are wrong, Lady Sara. An assassin only kills where there is profit to be made from the death. This plague kills without a care for fortune or honour or virtue. It cannot be stopped. Whereas an assassin is mortal – we sicken and die like anyone else. As will you, if you change your mind and stay here instead of coming with us to this monastery."

For a moment, she longed to stay. This was home, and perhaps she could help those who were sick. The plague couldn't kill everyone.

"Don't even think about it, Lady Sara. I'll throw you over my shoulder and carry you all the way up the mountain myself."

Before she could stop it, a giggle escaped from her lips. She'd heard tales of barbarians in far-off lands who carried women away like that, but she found it hard to believe that this assassin, whose courtly bow was a thing of beauty, could be anything like those savages.

She regained her composure, hoping he hadn't heard her silly giggle. "If you plan to carry me, how will you protect my son? Really, Master Zoticus, you are the strangest assassin I've ever met." She swept past him to take the pony's bridle, urging the creature to start pulling the cart toward the road.

She thought he heard him mutter something, half under his breath, but she couldn't make it out, so she dismissed it as not important.

Not when they had a camp to reach before nightfall, and a long journey ahead of them.

Twenty-Five

"Stubborn woman," Zoticus muttered under his breath as Sara set off with the cart. He said it again when he saw her making the rounds of all the children, speaking to every single one, before she allowed herself to rest for the night, though he could see how exhausted she was. She'd given her cloak to a child who had none, refusing to let the child return it. She was the last to eat every night, though she was the one preparing the meals. And more than once, he'd caught her milking the goats in the morning, to make sure everyone had some milk with breakfast before they started travelling for the day.

The journey was torturously slow. They barely covered a third of the distance Zoticus alone would have done in a day, and sometimes even less than that. Between the smaller children and the goats, it would likely be well into autumn when they arrived at the monastery, but Sara would not countenance the suggestion that any of them be left behind.

She was the sort of lady any barony would beg for. Without servants or a husband, she saw to the needs of everyone in her care. Yet to everyone except her son, she was Mistress Sara, without her proper title, because they saw her as one of their own.

When she was so much more.

They'd been travelling a week when the road grew steeper, headed into the mountains proper, and it took all his concentration to keep the pony headed up the road, instead of stopping or turning around and heading home, which is what the silly creature wanted. This was why Zoticus didn't own a horse. Not because he couldn't afford one, but because relying on a creature with a mind and will of its own was a recipe for disaster. That, and once he'd ridden Godfrey's divine mare, Pegasus, every other horse seemed as slow as this grumpy pony.

The next day, the road grew steeper still, and the miller's girl almost tripped over her own feet as she ran to him.

"Master Zoticus, it's Mistress Sara. She's fallen behind," the girl gasped out.

"You take the cart. I'll see to Lady Sara," he said, heading off.

He found her at the very back of their procession, leaning heavily on a goat that did not appreciate being anyone's crutch.

"Lady Sara, are you all right?" he asked carefully.

"I'm fine. Didn't sleep well last night, is all. I think there was a particularly sharp stone under my back that I couldn't seem to dislodge. I'm fine."

The goat took advantage of her distraction to bolt toward its fellows, higher up the hill, heedless of Lady Sara, who would have landed in the dust if not for Zoticus, who swooped in to catch her.

Then she began to cough.

"Lady Sara…" he began, not sure how to say what he dreaded.

"I'm fine. I just breathed in some of the dust that stupid beast kicked up when it ran away, is all. I'll just take a drink and be fine."

He handed her his flask.

While she drank, he palmed his healing amulet. He'd surreptitiously used it to scan each of the children in turn, relieved when their blood had shown no signs of the plague, but somehow he'd never checked Lady Sara. Now, it might be too late.

He pressed his thumb to one of the sharp claws holding the green stone in place, hissing as he felt it break the skin. A drop of blood was the price of certainty, and with Lady Sara, he needed to be certain. She had to reach the monastery on the mountain to realise his vision. She couldn't possibly have the plague. She couldn't.

He touched the amulet to her side. To heal her, it was best to have skin contact, but to simply see what ailed her, her dress would not impede his diagnosis.

"Please don't let it be the plague," he prayed silently as he searched her blood for signs of the dreaded pestilence. No, and no and no – it wasn't there.

Only then did he allow himself to breathe again. As always, Lady Sara was right. She was fine.

But just to make sure…

He lifted her off her feet and carried her to the nearest cart. "You shall ride up here for the rest of the day."

"I can walk just fine," she protested.

"That may be, but you didn't see that goat's expression. I'm sure he's not far away, plotting vengeance with all the other goats. You'll be safe from him and his friends up here, where he can't reach you," Zoticus said.

"I'm not afraid of my own goats!"

"Stubborn woman," he muttered.

Thankfully, she didn't hear him that time, either.

Twenty-Six

Zoticus didn't need to say it, but she knew he suspected it, as surely as she did. Once she'd started coughing, it was only a matter of time before she died of the plague. She kept herself apart from the others, mindful that the disease could be spread from one person to another, and she did not want any of their deaths on her conscience. Not when she would likely die soon herself.

She rode in a cart now, instead of walking alongside it. No one said a word, but she could feel Zoticus watching her. Waiting for her to die?

She wished she had let him seduce her, that first night in camp. One last memory, to take with her into whatever came next. Instead, she'd die wondering whether Tola was right…or whether he'd prove to be a good lover after all.

"Lady Sara!"

She almost thought she could feel his arms around her, laying her down, loosening the lacing on her gown, preparing to make love to her.

If this was to be her last thought on this earth, then at least it was a most wondrous dream.

Twenty-Seven

They rounded a bend and Zoticus took his eyes off Sara for a moment to take in the sight of the mountain monastery, the castle from his vision.

It soared above them, clinging to the cliffside like some sort of magical creation, ruling over the world. Thank heaven the gates were open, because the place would be nigh impregnable if they were shut.

A slight cough drew his eyes back to Sara. She toppled sideways in her seat, ending up slumped against a barrel that was all that kept her from tumbling out of the cart altogether.

Zoticus called for a halt. He lifted her out of the cart, not caring about anything but her right now. The kids – goat and human alike – parted to let him through.

He marched into the castle bailey, shouting for a healer.

But no one came.

He shouldered his way through the doors to the great hall, still shouting for help, but there was not even a fire lit there, though someone had laid one in readiness. He tugged off his cloak and spread it out on the flagstone floor, before laying Sara gently on the fur.

He lit the fire, making sure it was well alight before he dared to take his eyes off it. Sara needed warmth and healing, and he wasn't sure he was powerful enough to help her.

The children had followed him inside the hall, and some approached the fire, holding their hands out to warm them.

They were alive because of her. They owed her.

"Search the castle. See if you can find someone, anyone. Lady Sara needs a healer," he said.

Tobias, Raphael, Silvana, and many of the other older children spread out to obey his orders. The younger ones just stood around and looked lost.

For the first time in he couldn't remember how long, Zoticus knew exactly what that felt like.

Sara coughed weakly, her breath rasping in her throat.

He untied the lacing on her gown, hoping that would help her breathe, but still she struggled.

"I need a healer!" he howled, hoping whoever was here in the monastery would hear him and come help.

"I haven't found a healer, but I have found the best bedchamber. Mistress Sara will be more comfortable in a bed than here on the floor."

Zoticus stared around, looking for the source of the voice. Silvana, the miller's girl. He'd learned her name and others on the journey, but now he could scarcely remember his own name.

"Is there a fire there?" he demanded.

"I lit it myself, before I came down here. The bed could probably do with an airing, but if we stoke the fire hot enough, that should at least drive away the damp air." Silvana beckoned. "Bring her."

Zoticus bundled Sara up in his cloak and followed the girl.

The feather bed was piled high with furs. The fire had done little more than take the chill out of the air, so he set Sara down and proceeded to wrap her warmly.

"What else can I do for her?" Silvana asked.

"Find her a healer," he said.

She nodded and left.

An eternity passed while Zoticus held Sara in his arms. Her breathing was loud, but as long as she still drew breath, he could help her. He hoped.

"There's no one here. The whole place is empty. I've brought Raphael." Silvana shoved the boy forward. "Now I'm going to see if I can get the kitchen fire started, so we can cook something hot for dinner."

Raphael, the apothecary's apprentice, stood

awkwardly beside the bed. "I found the stillroom. There are many herbs hung up there, most of which I recognise, and shelves full of jars that could contain anything. It will take some time, but within a few days, I should be able to make something to help Mistress Sara. What would be best for her cough is oil of rue, but that will take weeks…"

Oil of rue. Hadn't the witch's girl sold him some?

Zoticus reached into his pouch, and the vial materialised in his hand.

"Only a few drops," he muttered to himself, holding the vial over her lips. Carefully, he counted out three drops before corking the vial again.

The boy was still there.

"Do what you can," Zoticus said. "I have enough oil of rue to do for some days yet."

Raphael left.

Zoticus pulled his healing amulet from beneath his tunic. He sliced his thumb open again, smearing blood across the stone, before touching the amulet to Sara's throat.

This time, he wasn't looking for plague. He

wanted to know what ailed her, in the faint hope that he might be able to fix it.

Her throat was inflamed, but the infection went deeper, coating the passageways carrying air to her lungs. No wonder she had so much trouble breathing. If he could but lessen the inflammation…

"Master Zoticus, you're bleeding on my mother's gown."

Zoticus palmed the amulet as he rose from the bed to face Tobias. The boy's face was pale.

"Is Mother…is she…?"

"She lives, though she is very ill. Perhaps now we are no longer travelling, she will be able to rest and recover," Zoticus said.

The boy nodded feverishly. "Good. Very good. For a moment there, I thought…" He shook his head. "Is it the plague?"

"No! I think she took a chill, and the rigours of travel made it worse," Zoticus said.

"Some of the girls have found the kitchen, and they say they will prepare dinner for everyone. The younger children have found what we think is the monks' dormitory, and they are busy bringing in straw for the beds so that we might sleep there. There is a sort of village green where I have left the goats, but I will have to milk them before the sun sets. The carts...." Tobias continued, but Zoticus stopped listening.

He'd brought them here because he'd seen Sara in his vision, running across the bailey, and nothing else mattered but her. She had to recover, because she still had to appear in his vision…

Tobias had finished talking, and he appeared to expect a response.

"Good, good," Zoticus said. "See that everyone eats and gets some rest, and ask the kitchen to send up some broth for Lady Sara."

When the boy had gone, Zoticus set the healing amulet to work again. He wasn't certain, but he thought the swelling in her throat had lessened a little. Just a little more, and she might find it easier to breathe.

For the first time in his life, he wished his mother were here with him. With the powerful magic running through her veins, a single drop of her blood would heal Sara in a matter of moments.

But he was all Sara had, so he'd do his best. Hoping that she'd wake up, and thank him, so he could deliver that terrible line about being honoured to be of service, and see desire burn in her eyes. Or maybe it was just irritation.

Right now, he'd settle for seeing her eyes open.

But they didn't open at all again that day, or during the night.

Twenty-Eight

Slowly, Sara became aware of voices. There was Tobias, Silvana and occasionally Raphael, always talking in hushed tones so that she could not always make out the words. Regret smote her – had she passed the plague on to them, too, so they were all dead? Served her right for trusting an assassin with her son's life. For the first time, she wondered if he'd receive a bonus for killing her, too, or whether that was always part of his plan. Or the plan of whoever had sent him. The Bishop of Rialto, most likely, who had always coveted the rich lands around the monastery. If they were all dead, then the lands would fall to him.

There was someone else there, too. Someone who moved silently, never said a word, and smelled strongly of rue and other medicinal herbs. One of the monks, preparing her body for burial? She wished she could have told him she'd prefer for her body to lie beside her husband's, in the churchyard in Mirroten, but she knew as well as anyone that the dead could not talk, let alone make their wishes known.

At least the strong-smelling monk didn't leave her. It was comforting to know that she was not alone. Perhaps that was why it was customary to hold a vigil before a funeral – if the soul had not yet been taken to heaven or hell or wherever they went in between, the loneliness was enough to overwhelm them.

Well, it threatened to overwhelm her. Only the scent of the monk and the gentle touch of his hands kept her from screaming out into the void she'd found herself in. No bishop should be able to steal her boy's birthright.

And then one day, the voices were no

longer quiet.

"It is unseemly that you are alone with her, when she is so vulnerable. She is a virtuous widow. Were she well, I know she would not allow you to enter her bedchamber. I have been remiss in my duties to my mother to allow it to go on so long. But it must stop." That was Tobias, speaking with unaccustomed authority. She hoped whoever he was speaking to could not detect the nervousness in his tone.

"Would you rather I did not heal her? She has been very ill, nigh unto death. If I had not been here, nor would she."

It took her a long moment to place the second voice, because she wasn't as familiar with it as her son's, but those smooth tones could only belong to Zoticus the assassin.

"I am grateful for your assistance, Master Zoticus, and will happily pay you for your healing services. That someone like you has such skills came as a pleasant surprise, but your services are not required here any more. As you say, she is improving, and will wake soon. What will it do to her, if the first thing she sees when she wakes is an assassin? I will not have her frightened. You must go. Raphael can heal her now."

A pause. "Perhaps we should take this discussion outside her chamber. Lady Sara needs her rest. I would not wish her to wake to heated words when she has suffered enough."

Footsteps and the sound of a door closing. The scrape of a bar being laid across the door, too, if she was not mistaken. Tobias was taking no chances that anyone would enter her room. The door must have been well made, for she could not hear their conversation, if it continued at all, once the door was closed.

Then Zoticus's words hit her. Nigh unto death.

Near, but not quite. She was alive.

A flood of feelings overwhelmed her. Regret at not seeing her husband again soon. Joy that she might see and speak to her son again. Anticipation, that she might thank Zoticus for whatever it was he had done. And uneasiness, because he'd said there was no cure for the plague. So whatever he'd done for her, it would surely come at great cost…

The scent of rue assailed her nostrils again. The monk was still there.

He would know what Zoticus had done, surely, for the monk never left. He would have seen all.

"Tell me, by what miracle have I survived the plague?" she asked softly.

Gentle laughter was his first response. "There are no miracles here. You survived because you left Mirroten before you were infected, along with the young people you commanded me to save. You fell ill because you took a chill, I believe, likely the night you spent with me in the forest. Travelling took its toll, and infection set in. Stubborn woman that you are, you hid your weakness well, so that the infection was far advanced by the time we arrived here at the Cloister. Healing you…that took magic, I'm afraid. But I will show you if you wish."

She opened her eyes. Zoticus stood before her, clasping something in his hands that she could not see. She scanned the room, and was surprised to find that they were alone. "Where is the monk?" she asked.

"There are no monks. The Cloister was deserted when we arrived, and none have returned from their quest for plague survivors. I last saw them in Altino, burying the dead. It is possibly none of them will return, for corpses carry the plague, too."

She took a moment to digest this. No monks, and Tobias had said Zoticus was her healer. She reached for his hand, which he allowed her to bring to her nose. Sara inhaled deeply, once, twice, three times, just to make sure. "You smell of rue," she said.

"Oil of rue helps to ease a cough, like yours. It has also been known to bring on visions of the future, and I hoped…" He shook his head.

"What did you see of my future, Master Zoticus?" she asked, curious.

He pulled his hand from her grasp and looked away. "I saw nothing I did not already know."

Evasion. Interesting. She would ask him again later. Other questions burned more brightly on her tongue.

"And what of my son?" She'd heard his voice only a short time ago, so curiosity and not worry fuelled this question, too.

He smiled. "Your son is snoring, asleep outside your door. He is not a particularly effective guard, but he is a dutiful son. No one can unbar your door without waking him, so you may sleep soundly."

"Yet how are you here?"

He spread his hands wide. "An assassin has many secrets. Surely you do not expect me to share them all?"

She folded her arms across her chest. "Only this one."

He jerked his thumb at the wall hanging behind him. "There's a servants' stair behind that tapestry. It comes out near the kitchen, hidden behind another tapestry."

She nodded. "So if I asked you to bring me dinner, you would be faster than anyone else, who would have to convince my son to unbar the door first?"

He laughed. "If you're hungry, that is a very good sign. I admit I am not as good a healer as I am an assassin, so to know that I have successfully healed you is…most gratifying."

"You said you would show me how you'd

healed me," she said slowly. "Tola said you might have magic. Is it true?"

"Now that is a secret I have never shared outside my family," he said.

She'd known Tola long enough to hear how magical bloodlines worked. "That's because they have magic, too." She fixed him with her gaze. "You said you would show me if I wish. Well, I do wish."

His courtly bow made her smile. She'd never thought to see it again. "As my lady desires."

He thrust out his hand, as if to seize her breast.

Suddenly she became aware that she was only wearing a thin shift, and not the one she'd been wearing on the road. This one was cut so low, if she leaned forward, her breasts would spill out.

"Did you undress me?" she demanded.

He stepped back, dropping his hands by his sides. "I did consider it, but the miller's girl, Silvana, took your clothes for laundering. When I returned, I found you wearing a fresh shift. Should you wish to change again, I'd be more than happy to assist you. I'm not unfamiliar with helping women out of their clothes."

A few of those courtly bows, a smile just like the cheeky one he wore now, a handful of courtly compliments delivered in that cultured voice so deep she felt its vibration in her belly…he wouldn't have to lift a finger before women removed their clothes for him.

There was a definite question in his eyes, now, too. After all, she was lying in an enormous bed in nothing but a thin shift. It would only take a word for him to join her. If only her breath hadn't caught in her throat…

She blinked and that look in his eyes was gone.

"You're still not quite well, Lady Sara. You did say you wished to see how I heal you."

She eyed his hand, once again headed for her breast. She still couldn't see what he held in it. "Perhaps you should tell me first."

He flipped his hand over, and showed her the amulet resting on his palm. A cloudy green stone, framed in an ornate silver setting. A thick leather thong dangled from it, as though he normally wore it around his neck.

"This is a healing amulet, given to me many years ago by a powerful enchantress. Its healing powers are activated by my blood, and my blood alone. While I wear it on my person, it helps my body to heal faster, saving me from many a wound that might have been mortal, and destroying diseases, including the plague, when they come into contact with my blood."

Sara nodded slowly. "So it has a price, this healing amulet of yours. The magic in your blood. The witch who gave it to you must have been very wise."

Zoticus smiled. "That she is. What she did not tell me is that I might use it to heal others, too, but as you have already guessed, it comes at a price. A blood price. The magic in my blood activates the amulet's healing powers, but the amulet must be close to the person I wish to heal. The magic is strongest when it rests against the skin, near the wound or sickness. So for your infection, I would place it over your heart, or at your throat."

Only a fool allowed an assassin anywhere near their throat. Then again, Sara suspected he posed even more danger to her heart.

"You're the healer, Master Zoticus. Where will it do the most good?"

Twenty-Nine

If he placed his hand at her throat, he knew he would cup her face and kiss her. If he put his hand on her chest, though, he'd have to remain rigidly in control, concentrating only on healing her and not the deliciously soft flesh beneath his fingers.

"I would prefer your heart," he said without a word of a lie.

But then he had to swallow manfully as she pulled the neckline of her shift down to expose half her breast. By all that was holy, he wanted…

"Please heal me," she whispered.

Zoticus shook himself. He'd never been this distracted by a woman, not since before he became an assassin.

He took a knife and sliced open his palm, then laid it atop the amulet. The stinging pain helped him concentrate on what he should be doing, and not anything else.

The swelling in her throat had gone down, but the infection still lingered in her blood and in her airways. He focussed on burning it out of her blood and the rest of her body, until none of it remained.

There. It was done.

Gasping, he pulled away from her, and the amulet tumbled to the floor.

He dropped to his knees, feeling for it in the darkness, for the fire had died down to embers. He'd been healing her for a long time.

Pain pierced his hand, and he drew the amulet out from under the bed. It was a thirsty thing, but worth the blood price he'd paid for healing her. He'd do it again, even if Sara had been infected with the plague instead of some simple infection.

"It's done. You're completely healed, Lady Sara," he said. "Your body will still be weak as you recover, but the illness is gone."

He headed for the fireplace, so that he might mend her fire before he left.

"How did a man like you become an assassin, Master Zoticus?" she asked.

He had yet to meet another man even remotely like himself, but he did not correct her. "It was so long ago, I scarcely remember," he lied.

"Please try," she said. "Because you've spent years shedding blood for a living, and tonight you've shed yours to save my life. I want to understand how you can."

He stayed silent for a long moment, determined to fix her fire. Far too soon, it was again blazing merrily, licking at a fresh log.

"I have a twin sister. Now, she's a powerful enchantress in her own right, while there isn't enough magic in my blood to cast a spell without an enchanted object to focus it. So she used her elemental magic as easily as breathing, while I spent most of my time in the woods around where we lived. Our mother was the village witch, much like your friend Tola, so I would hunt and trap in the forest, and bring back meat for our table.

"One day, my sister's friend went missing. We were not much older than your son Tobias, but everyone else our age was settling down and getting married, having children. All except us and her friend, Amice.

"Now, Amice was fond of stories, and there are plenty of them, telling how some brave, noble knight or lord or prince finds a girl in the woods, saves her from something fearful, and makes her his wife. It was no secret that Amice dreamed of marrying a knight, at the very least.

"And it so happened that a party of knights came to our town, on their way to a tourney of some sort, but they intended to break the monotony of their journey with some hunting.

"A few days after their arrival, Amice went missing. And my sister, who could level a castle, drain a lake or stir up a storm so strong it could blow a grown man down, could not find out where the girl had gone. So she asked me to track her, and I did.

"It took me hours, but I tracked her to a camp where the knights had spent the night. But the camp was empty, and the only prints I found leaving the camp were all from horses' hooves. So when Amice left the camp, it had to be on horseback."

"Oh, the poor girl!" Sara said.

Zoticus shook his head. "Oh, she was willing enough, I wager. She wanted to marry a knight, and she'd found a whole company of them. She'd have her pick and live happily ever after, or so I thought. So I went home to tell my sister.

"My sister, who'd seen more of the world than me at that point, being an enchantress and all, feared even more for her friend. She knew not all knights and noblemen were honourable, and even if these ones were, she still wanted to make sure her friend was happy. So she sent me off after them."

He sucked in a breath. Should he tell her, or not? His instincts told him yes.

"That night, I had my first vision, though I thought it a dream at the time. I saw Amice in the forest, lying in a pool of blood. Even thinking it was a dream, it was enough to spur me on after her.

"Now, this was a mounted hunting party. They followed whatever prey took their fancy, which led them a merry chase. I was a boy on foot, following their tracks. But I knew they were going to a tourney, and when they got there, they would stay for some time, so I kept on following those tracks, hoping I would find them eventually.

"They stopped to camp and roast a deer they'd caught. When I found their camp, they could not have been gone a day. But the knights were all gone. Only Amice remained.

"I didn't see her at first. She was huddled in the bushes, weeping, and when she saw me, she tried to hide. Of course, I hadn't tracked her over so many miles to be fooled by a few leaves, so I pulled her out and begged her to tell me what was wrong.

"Her story started out like any of the tales she loved. The knights fought an impromptu battle for the honour of sitting beside her, and the winner…well, I don't know if it was that night or later, but he took her into his bed, telling her all manner of stories about how much he loved her and wanted her for his wife. For a few weeks, she was completely under his spell…until they approached the town where the tourney was to be held, not a day's ride from where I'd found her.

"On the last day, after he'd satisfied his lust, her seducer told her he no longer loved her, and they all rode off, leaving her there.

"I was horrified by her tale, but offered to take her home. That only made her cry harder, until she produced a knife and stabbed herself in the chest. Then she tore the knife out of her breast and flung it across the clearing. By some terrible mischance, she'd pierced her heart, and there was no saving her. Within minutes, my vision lay before me — her body in a pool of blood in a forest clearing."

"Did you love her terribly?" Sara whispered.

Zoticus laughed. "Amice? By all that's holy, no! She was Zoraida's best friend, and if I so much as thought about kissing her, my sister had promised she'd set fire to my bed. Oh, my life would have been so much simpler if I'd fallen in love with Amice. Then, I'd never been in love in my life, and the village girls knew me as the enchantress's twin brother, son to the village witch, with no magic of my own. As far as eligible bachelors go, I think I was just above the pig boy, and that was only because I was better looking."

Sara smiled faintly. "Were you more modest then, too?"

"Heavens, no! If anything, I thought I was invincible. Like most boys that age do. So I swore on Amice's body that I would seek vengeance for her lost honour. A boy against trained tourney knights. I was a hunter, not a fighter. I must have lost my mind.

"Luckily, by the time I reached the tourney grounds, I'd regained my wits, and instead of challenging them or something else equally stupid, I filled a vacancy for a stable boy at the inn where they were staying. I listened to the gossip, watched the tourneys, and soon worked out that I was no match for any of the knights. Worse, the one who'd seduced Amice had a new bedwarmer, and the girl could not have been more than twelve years old!

"When the tourney was over, I attached

myself to Sir Seducer's party as a groom. We hadn't been riding long before I discovered that not only did the man pick up a new maiden to deflower in every town, but he had a wife at home, waiting for him.

"Now, I'd grown up with enchantresses. I knew women ruled the world, and I thought my best chance would be to tell the knight's wife about his crimes. Until I met the girl."

Zoticus took a deep breath. "Lady Gemma was the most exquisite girl you'd ever seen. She looked like an angel, and she could not have been a day older than I was. Younger, perhaps, in years, but not when it came to the ways of the world. She had eyes as pale and hard as twin diamonds. Because unlike the peasant girls her husband had seduced, Lady Gemma's father was a knight, who'd insisted upon marriage between his daughter and his fellow knight. Whether money changed hands or they were just very drunk, I know not, but Lady Gemma only warmed her husband's bed for a few weeks, before he tired of her and returned to seducing innocents like Amice.

"Lady Gemma also wanted vengeance on

her husband. And she began by taking her husband's newest groom into her bed."

Sara's jaw dropped.

She really was the virtuous widow her son thought she was, if that shocked her.

"Lady Gemma, young though she was, ruled her husband's estate. He was off chasing virgins or tourneys or deer for most of the year, so she grew accustomed to giving orders and having them obeyed. And she was no different in the bedchamber. It turned out I was not her first lover, and she was most particular about how she wished to be made love to.

"At first, I thought it was a fitting fate for Sir Seducer to learn his wife had lost her heart to me, as Amice had to him. But as I became more familiar with every bit of Lady Gemma's body, I soon learned that she had no heart…and that she was inexorably winning my own.

"How could I not think myself in love with her? She insisted we make love multiple times a night, pleasuring her in between, and if the other grooms found me asleep in the hayloft after another strenuous night, they just muttered that I was Lady Gemma's lover, and let me go back to sleep.

"This went on for some months, until one night Lady Gemma claimed to be ill, and banished me from her bed. The next morning, a servant brought a message from her that she wished me to deliver a letter to her husband, wherever he might be, and to attend her in her chambers that night.

"Any hopes I'd had of sharing her bed again before I left were dashed when she greeted me with the letter I was to carry, and a whispered promise that she would consider taking me into her bed again if I were to make sure her husband never came home, so she'd be free to marry again.

"And, like the fool I was, I believed her.

"When I caught up with Sir Seducer – I cannot remember his name, for all my names for him were epithets then – it was at the start of another hunting expedition. I joined the other servants, and waited for my opportunity. I had never killed a man before, but I was determined to do this for Amice and Lady

Gemma.

"Sir Seducer shot a stag, then dismounted so that he might finish it off. The other knights had started chasing another target, so he was alone.

"Then, the only enchanted object I owned was my flute, the same one I used to summon the rats in Mirroten. That day, I used it to bring a boar. The beast gored Sir Seducer in the back, and then gored him again as he lay writhing on the ground. His friends heard his screams and came to help, but there was nothing anyone could do. He died in agony, several days later, and I was jubilant when I headed home to tell the good news to Lady Gemma."

Years had passed, but he never forgot that day. He'd been such a fool.

"She was at dinner when I arrived, and I had to deliver my news to her in the great hall, standing below her on the dais. She ordered that the house be placed in mourning, and dismissed me. Me!

"That night, I went to her bedchamber, just like I used to do, only to discover that it had been turned into a nursery. The bedchamber where I'd made love to Lady Gemma all those nights now belonged to twin boys, so tiny they could not have been long out of the womb. The boys' wet nurses stared at me until one of them had the presence of mind to direct me to Lady Gemma's new chamber.

"There, I learned that the boys were now Sir Seducer's heirs, though the knight had not shared her bed in years, and she would rule in their stead until the boys came of age. All the servants, of course, would swear to the boys' legitimacy, for they were hers, heart and soul.

"I delighted at the thought that my sons — for who else could be their father? — would have lands of their own and knightly titles. I promised her I would train them well, and spend every day teaching them to be better men than her now dead husband. And my nights would be hers, of course, as was her right.

"She merely laughed, tossed a pouch of coins on the floor at my feet, and said if I ever breathed a word about our arrangement or attempted to see the boys again, she would hire a real assassin to hunt me down and silence me forever. And so…I went home."

After a considerable amount of time begging Lady Gemma to change her mind, Zoticus thought but did not say. Lady Sara already thought he'd been foolish. She did not need to know the entire extent of his idiocy.

But her eyes were wide over the hand she'd used to cover her mouth. "How old were you?"

"When I went home, I was a few weeks shy of my eighteenth birthday. I spent more than a year in Lady Gemma's service."

"Have you seen your boys again?"

Zoticus grinned. "Several times. They both became knights, and while they do occasionally host tourneys, now they have come into their inheritance, they are far too busy managing the vast estate Lady Gemma amassed from her four former husbands to waste as much time on such things as Sir Seducer."

"Do they know you're their father?"

"No! Lady Gemma gave them plenty of father figures, before she chose widowhood again. She contracted some other assassin for the other husbands, as I would not take the contract."

"Did you regret killing the first knight?"

Zoticus hesitated. He suspected most people regretted their first kill, but he never did. "No. He preyed upon children, and felt no guilt for his actions. How many more girls like Amice and Gemma would he have harmed if I had let him live? Death was too good for him, but it was the only justice I could give them, so I did. If Lady Gemma came to me now and asked me to kill her first husband, I would still do it."

"Do you still love her?"

This time, there was no hesitation. "No. I don't think I ever truly did. I was in love with the idea of a woman who wanted me in her bed every night. A boy's brain is in the head of his cock at that age, as I'm sure you know."

Sara snorted with laughter, which sent her into a coughing fit. Zoticus leaped to grab the potion that soothed her throat, which he'd been keeping warm on the hearth.

He helped her sit up so that she could drink, and when she finally had the breath to speak again, she was so close…

"Have you ever loved a woman?"

"Yes." And he'd give everything he owned to lie her down and make love to her right now, but her son was right. She was vulnerable after being so sick, and he had no right to take advantage of this virtuous widow.

So he bade her good night, and took the servants' stairs up to the small chamber he'd claimed as his own.

<h1 style="text-align:center">Thirty</h1>

"Open the door, this is heavy!"

Sara woke in daylight to shouts in the passage outside her door. Though she'd been utterly exhausted from Zoticus's healing and whatever the sickness had done to her body, she'd lain awake for far too long last night, her mind churning through all the things he'd said.

He was an assassin, a rat catcher, a hero, a healer, a flirt…he'd been sixteen or seventeen, the same age as Tobias, when fate had turned him into….not so much an assassin as a vigilante. He'd gone after justice, killing a knight for crimes he'd committed, and only circumstances and the horrid Lady Gemma had turned him into an assassin, after the fact.

Such a horrible, heartbreaking story, that she wanted to be fiction, but he'd told it without leaving out his own foolishness, so she knew it had to be true.

He'd brought them here, to the Cloister of Holy Innocents, and healed her with his own blood.

Her thoughts darted back to that first day he'd appeared in the council hall, when he'd announced that he'd save the town from the plague.

He might not have saved everyone in town, but he'd saved enough of them. He'd said that night in the forest that he wouldn't lie to her. Had everything he said been the truth, even when she doubted him?

The door to her chamber burst open, and a parade of people came in.

First came Zoticus with an enormous wooden tub, like a larger version of the one they used to crush the chestnut shells. He set it down before the fire and waved the next person through. The rest were children, each carrying a bucket of water, which they sloshed into the tub. Then they headed out again.

"Four buckets each, and then you may go to the kitchens to get your apple from Sal!" he shouted after them.

"Master Zoticus, my mother is not well. You shouldn't shout like that in here," Tobias said.

Zoticus bowed in her direction. "My deepest apologies, Lady Sara. Now, how would you like me to shout at the children bringing water for your bath?"

Poor Tobias looked lost. He'd spent all his life herding goats and learning to lead the people of Mirroten, but Zoticus was outside of anything he'd ever had to deal with before. Even Sara wasn't sure how to handle him, especially after last night. But she knew she definitely wanted to.

"Your cheeks look flushed, Mother. Has your fever returned? Or is it too hot in here? Should I bank the fire? Or send Raphael down to the stillroom for some medicine? Or are you thirsty? I can send down to the kitchen for some goat's milk…"

"I'm fine. Truly, Tobias. Master Zoticus has taken good care of me. Who knew he had such healing skills? I am still tired today, but perhaps tomorrow I will be well enough to leave my bed. Don't worry about me." She managed a smile, hoping her cheeks had cooled. "I'll ask one of the children to bring me something from the kitchen to break my fast. I'm sure you have more important things to do."

He wrinkled his nose. "I've been trying to teach a few of them to take care of the goats. They're slowly grasping the idea that they must watch them all the time, but teaching them to milk the goats so far has been a disaster. Was I ever so fumble-fingered?"

"Well, you did learn young. As soon as you could walk, you wanted to help with the milking. It takes time and practice. Then again, perhaps your new goatherds simply don't have the right touch for milking. See if you can find some of the children who came from families that owned goats, and whose job it was to do the milking. Even if it's just to help teach the others, with extra skilled hands, the milking will go faster."

Tobias nodded. "Thank you, Mother. It's good to see you well again. I don't know how we've managed without you."

Zoticus stepped forward. "You'll have to manage for some time longer before Lady Sara is truly well again. She still needs rest."

Tobias opened his mouth to argue, but the bucket brigade had returned, and the noisy splashing and clattering as the children filled the bath up further prevented all conversation.

When they were gone, Sara got in first. "I still am terribly tired, Tobias. All I seem to want to do is sleep!"

"Your body needs sleep to heal. It's only natural. Once the children are done bringing up water for your bath, you should sleep again. The water can warm by the fire while you sleep, so it will be ready for you when you wake. In the meantime, I'll go down to the kitchen and fetch you some food." Zoticus bowed again, then departed.

Tobias waited a moment, then dropped his voice. "Mother, are you sure we can trust him?

Father Fazzio said he's an assassin, and he has committed so many terrible crimes, the only way he can earn forgiveness for them is to go on a holy crusade. I fear for your life, leaving you alone with him."

Yet Sara had no such qualms. Not any more.

"He has healed me of his own volition, when he had plenty of opportunities to do me harm, yet he did not. He has already been on a crusade, which is more than Father Fazzio has, so I'm not sure the priest is any position to judge him. If Zoticus has a heavy conscience, then that is his burden to bear. He will be judged for his sins at the end of his life, as will we all. Rumours abound about his actions in the past, but who is to say any of it is more than common gossip? What I've seen of his actions since I've met him show him to be selfless, and somewhat of a hero. He saved my life, but he also saved all of us from the plague. We all should be grateful to him, you more than anyone."

"How can you be sure he didn't bring the plague to Mirroten?" Tobias persisted.

Sara considered for a long moment. She couldn't truly be certain but… "Anyone who comes into contact with the plague falls ill. Ysabel was ill before Zoticus arrived, yet Zoticus has showed no signs of illness. He's survived the plague before, but he was still very ill. No, the plague arrived before he did. Before Father Fazzio received word from his bishop about Altino. It must have been Mercurio. Zoticus said he'd seen Mercurio's ship on his way to Mirroten, and Mercurio was already dead of the plague. The hay he brought from Altino must have been tainted. I remember Ysabel and her father saying the first thing they would do with it was to restuff their mattresses…" She closed her eyes. "Poor Ysabel. Ahab wanted you to marry her, when she was old enough, you know."

Tobias edged away from her, as he always did when talk turned to marriage. "I have work to do, Mother. But it is good to see you recovering." When he reached the door, he hurried away.

When Sara could no longer hear his footsteps, the tapestry twitched aside and

Zoticus stepped into the room.

"You're wrong, you know. I bear part of the blame for the plague coming to your town, even if it arrived before me. When I returned from that accursed crusade, we boarded three ships at Byzas that had been left behind after a battle gone wrong. The rats aboard carried the plague, and few of us survived the voyage to Rialto. I asked one of the Rialto merchants, a man I trusted, to see that the tainted ships and their cargo were burned. Perhaps he forgot, or perhaps he was too greedy to give up what he saw as his, but he did not burn those ships. And when he died, his sons inherited them. Not knowing their history, they sold the ships and the cargo…to your river trader, Mercurio. So while I may not have carried the plague on my person to your town, I am not blameless in the matter. I should have burned those ships the day they arrived in Rialto. By the time I did burn them, it was too late."

"I should have been more outspoken at the town council meeting, and insisted we take precautions to keep the plague out of Mirroten, and prevent its spread. Instead, I let

Ahab overrule me, and allow trade to continue despite the risks. I knew the hay had come from Altino, and I could have commanded it to be burned, but it did not occur to me that it would be necessary until now. It was my duty to save Mirroten, and I failed. None of us are blameless in this, except maybe the children. Children you saved."

"I should have saved more."

"So should I. But we do what we can, try the best we can, and we'll never be able to save everyone." Sara sighed. "Perhaps you should have let me die instead of healing me. So many regrets…"

"No." Zoticus set his tray of food on the table beside her bed. "The moment I arrived in Mirroten, I knew I was not too late to save someone, at least. I knew you would survive the plague, but only if you left Mirroten."

"How…?"

He wet his lips. "I saw a vision of you. Here. Well, in the bailey here, not this bedchamber."

Sara paled. "You mean you saw me dead, like your friend Amice?"

"No. I saw you alive, very much alive. You

run across the bailey. That's all I see."

Relief trickled into her chest, making it easier to breathe again. "Then your vision won't happen today, as I feel far too weak to walk across this room, let alone run anywhere."

Zoticus smiled. "Ah, that I can help with. You should have some of this broth, while it's still warm, and then see if you can sleep again. You'll regain your strength faster while you're asleep."

"Will you be here when I wake?" She wasn't sure why it was so important to her, but it was.

"Where else would I be?"

Thirty-One

By the time Lady Sara woke again, her son had already barred her door for the night. If Zoticus had had any sense, he'd have stayed on the other side of that door, and let her bathe in peace.

But as he evidently had no sense, he gave in to his selfish desire to watch over her while she slept. After all, he had said he'd be there when she woke, and he valued her good opinion. Perhaps more than he should.

He'd set out supper for the two of them on the table and checked a dozen times to make sure the water was warm. He'd left a pile of stones on the hearth, ready to drop into her bath to heat the water even more when she was ready. He'd even brought out his enchanted candle, which warmed a room better than any fire could. He was taking no chances that she'd catch another chill.

Lady Sara's eyes fluttered open. She took in the room with a single glance, then said, "Alone at last." There was a throaty purr to her voice, just like she'd had on the day he met her. She really was recovering.

Zoticus bowed his head. "I will leave you alone to bathe, if you wish it." Though he hoped she didn't.

"Some healer you are. What if I am too weak to walk to the bath? Please stay and stand watch while a stubborn old woman washes."

He snorted. "You're not old, Lady Sara. You cannot be a day older than me."

"But I am stubborn. I see. Ooh, is that supper? Am I allowed to eat something before I have my bath?"

"If your appetite has returned, it's a very good sign. Yes, if you're hungry, you should eat." He eyed her for a moment. "Do you feel up to sitting at the table, or would you prefer to eat in bed?"

"I haven't spent this long in bed since I was a new bride."

His mouth gaped. Had she really said that?

Sara winked. "It was so much softer than rolling around in the pasture or the hayloft, and when there's no one to interrupt, you can take more time to really enjoy yourself." She glanced at the door. "I take it the door's barred again?"

"Yes. Though your son found a padlock to fasten it with today, too, so he could sleep in his own bed, instead of outside your chamber tonight."

"Was that your doing?"

Already she knew him too well.

"Perhaps. It might have just been a happy accident."

He shouldn't have done it. Without the boy listening outside the door, he might do something reckless…

"I think we should have supper at the table," she said, thankfully interrupting his thoughts before they went too far.

"Yes."

He carried her over to the table, and, for a time, they ate in silence. Zoticus finished his portion before she was halfway done with hers, so he headed for the hearth to heat up her bath. He used tongs to transfer the hot stones into the water, which hissed and steamed where the stones hit the surface. After a few minutes, he tested the temperature, then took out the stones. "The bath is ready when you are," he said.

A rustling sound behind him made him turn.

He could do nothing but stare.

She'd slipped out of her shift and stood naked beside her chair.

He'd never seen anything so beautiful in his life. He didn't have the words to describe her.

And then he did, just one: soft.

So soft he ached to touch her, kiss her, everywhere…

Which, of course, made him, her opposite, suddenly hard.

"I'll help you," he said, rushing to her side.

He lifted her up and carried her to the bath, then let her down gently into the water. He dropped to his knees beside the tub, hoping she hadn't noticed. Then his traitorous hand picked up the washcloth and he found himself asking, "What would you like me to wash first?"

What happened next he could only describe as pure agony. Stroking the soap and the cloth over her skin, reminding himself every moment that he was her healer, yet aware of her every breath, each time she closed her eyes, and every time she moved to grant him better access to her magnificent body. At least when he was on his knees, his tunic hid his erection.

"I think I'm clean now." She sounded regretful.

Now he had to help her out of the bath, dry her, and get her back to bed. Without her seeing that his mind was full of very un-healer-ish thoughts.

He held up the towel like a shield. "Climb out, then."

When she was finally back in bed, mercifully covered by the sheets, he tried to form an excuse so that he could escape before she saw.

"The water's still warm. You should have a bath, too," she said.

"Yes." His tongue had turned traitor, too.

Now he had no choice but to turn his back and take his clothes off.

Thirty-Two

Sara knew she was wicked to watch Zoticus undress and climb into the bath, particularly when her body was most definitely showing her age and held no attraction for him, but she wasn't getting any younger, and this might be her last chance to see a good looking man naked.

The muscles that had only been hinted at when hidden by his tunic were all on display now. She could see how he'd lifted her so easily. Yet he'd been so gentle when he handled her in the bath.

If he'd shown the slightest spark of interest, she'd happily invite him to share her bed. Actually, she wasn't above begging. She hadn't ached this badly for a man since…since…she could not remember.

"I can feel your eyes on me. What are you thinking?" he asked.

She wasn't sure whether she wanted to laugh or cry. "I was wishing I was a young maiden again, pretty and comely still, so that I might tempt you to come to my bed."

There. Let him think what he liked of her.

His shoulders hunched, then he turned to face her. "Lady Sara, I cannot believe that you have ever been more beautiful or irresistible than you are now." He slowly rose, and the water cascaded off him.

She couldn't stop staring.

"That looks painful," she managed to say.

"I've been thus…afflicted since you first took off your shift. I've never been so powerless to control myself since I was a boy."

Just the sight of him, jutting out so pointedly, made her braver. "Come to bed."

He began to dry himself. "I want to do that

more than anything, but I keep reminding myself how deathly ill you have been, that you are still weak, that I should not take advantage of you while you are so vulnerable. I'm first and foremost your healer, and you should be resting."

Sara smiled. "I promise not to leave the bed."

Zoticus muttered an oath, half under his breath.

He hung the damp towel over a chair, revealing the full glory of his naked body.

No, she was not too proud to beg. Not when they both wanted this.

"On the road, when I fainted, I thought I was dying. My last thought, my only regret, was that I hadn't had my way with you, that night we were alone in the forest camp."

He stared at her for a long moment. "I'm a fool. I should have told you that night that no one had commissioned me to kill your son. I didn't know the boy existed until you mentioned him, and I would never accept a contract for a child."

She should have been surprised, but she

wasn't. When she'd first heard he was an assassin, she'd put two and two together and arrived at a conclusion that simply wasn't possible. She would never have suspected such a thing of the man she knew now. The man who'd saved them all, including her. And that was only a part of why she wanted him so much.

She shrugged her shoulders and let the sheets fall away. She hadn't put a shift on after her bath, so now he could see everything, too. "We all have our moments of madness. Right now, I want to savour being alive, and celebrate how you saved me, and I want to do it all naked in bed with you."

She'd never imagined he could improve upon his courtly bow, but seeing him doing it naked was a memory she'd treasure. The way all those muscles bunched up just so…

"As my lady commands."

Thirty-Three

For a moment, she'd looked as nervous as a new bride. Then her expression had turned hungry as she'd talked of madness in that purring tone and Zoticus was lost.

He found himself kneeling between her thighs on the bed, a breath away from burying himself deep inside her.

"Yes," she whispered.

No. Once he was inside her, he wouldn't last more than a moment, and he might never have this chance again.

He leaned forward and captured her lips.

This kiss was slow and deliberate, nothing like that first one he'd stolen with barely a thought, before a vision had mercifully stopped him from going any further. But now, the only vision he saw was her half-lidded eyes, begging him for more even as she returned his kiss.

Her breasts were soft as silk in his hands, until her hardening nipples made their presence known. Only then did he release her lips, leaving a light trail of kisses down her neck and collarbone.

"I want to feel you inside me, Zoticus," she said.

He wanted that, too, but not yet.

He ran his hand down her belly, through her downy curls and then slid his finger inside her. He hooked it…

She cried out, arching her back.

His fingers worked their magic, but it was her breasts that had his attention now, thrust up toward him as they were. He sucked hard on the nearest nipple, was rewarded by her moan, and took his time on one breast, then the other, until he felt her clenching around his finger.

"Yes, yes…" she whispered.

No.

First, he wanted to give her the pleasure of an unforgettable kiss.

He lifted her legs over his shoulders, so they spread beautifully wide.

With both hands now, he parted her lower lips, seeing them glisten in the candlelight. If he'd been in any doubt that she wanted him…

"What are you doing? I want you inside me, not…looking at my…" She blushed, like a bride seeing her first cock.

"You'll see, Lady Sara. I promise you'll like it. Just as I like looking at you." And then his tongue was too busy for talking, too busy tasting, for his fingers had brought her to the brink and it only took a few strokes to tip her over…

Thirty-Four

Sara had barely a moment to realise that Zoticus had slipped his tongue inside her before sensation overwhelmed her, and all she could do was scream his name.

When she opened her eyes, she saw he'd risen onto his knees, lifting her legs with him.

"Why…" she began.

His hot, hard head entered her then, and she no longer cared why. All she cared about was the tortuously slow thrust as he filled her. She could scarcely breathe, he felt so good.

"Lady Sara, are you all right? Did I hurt

you?"

She opened her eyes to see his concern, but it took her a few swallows before she found her voice to respond.

"Heavens, no, but it's…so long…"

"Forgive me, did I go too deep? I shouldn't have…" He started to lower her legs, and it felt like he was starting to slip out of her.

"No! You're not too long. I mean it's so long since I've shared a bed, I'd forgotten it could be this good." Sara felt her face grow hot. "Please don't stop."

He laughed softly, then leaned forward to kiss her, pushing into her to the very hilt.

Oh, yes. She must have said it aloud, for he smiled and began to move, never taking his eyes off hers. He started off slow, but as passion kindled in his eyes, lit by the blaze between their joined bodies, each thrust became harder, faster, until she felt herself clenching around him, sucking in a breath to scream his name again.

"Oh God, Sara!"

They came at the same moment, the most exquisite pleasure marred only by its ending.

He covered her face and her breasts with kisses, still breathing hard. Then he threw himself down on the bed beside her.

"The second time will be slower, I promise," he said. "Slow and gentle, like I should've done the first time."

Her thighs still ached from the first time, and everything in between was tingling. Slow and gentle might be nice, too, but…

"Then the third time, I want hard and fast again," she said. As if anyone could make love three times in a single night.

Zoticus began to laugh. "And what does my lady command me to do on the fourth time we make love?"

"I don't know," she admitted, "but earlier, I had hoped you'd join me in the bath. Maybe…"

"Ah, speaking of baths, I should probably get us cleaned up." He produced a bowl and a wash cloth and proceeded to do just that. Until he started stroking the cloth between her thighs in just the right place, and she couldn't help but arch her back up…

The cloth splashed back into the bowl, to be

replaced by his fingers and the rasp of his hot tongue.

"And the fifth, my lady?" he asked. "And the sixth, and the seventh?"

His tongue rejoined his fingers and she could no longer think. All she wanted was him.

"Have me…however you like. As many times as possible. As long as…you don't…stop. Don't…stop…Zoticus! Oh my God!"

He was the very spirit of constancy, for he most certainly did not stop, though she screamed his name until she was hoarse. And she didn't want him to – not now, not ever.

One night would never be enough.

Thirty-Five

The next morning, Sara awoke to a light tap on her door. "Are you awake, Mother?" Tobias asked.

In panic, her eyes darted to the bed beside her, but Zoticus had already gone. Some hours ago, judging by how cold the sheets there were compared to last night. A pity. She wouldn't have minded one more round before breakfast…would it count as the eighth time in a night, if the sun had risen?

She really shouldn't be thinking such things with her son standing outside the door.

"Come in," she called.

Tobias shouldered his way through the door, carrying a tray with what she presumed was her breakfast on it. "I brought you something to eat, and a tisane from Raphael that he said will help you regain your strength."

It wouldn't be as potent as Zoticus's healing amulet, which he'd insisted on using on her again last night after the third time they'd made love, but she wouldn't refuse anything that might help her recover. She wanted many more nights like last night.

"Thank you," she said. "How did the milking go this morning?"

"A little better. With more people to show how it was done, instead of just me, we ended up with more milk in the buckets, less on the floor, and it was finished before breakfast, for the first time. Sal's been checking what provisions they have in the cellars here, and aside from a lot of cider, there isn't much to see them through the winter. There's an orchard of chestnut trees on the slopes below the monastery, and they're ready for harvest, so I set some of the boys the task of collecting nuts. Silvana said there's a smoke house beside the mill. It's not as big as ours, but it will give them something to do. She says she can operate the mill, too, if I find her a couple of hands to help. The apple trees will yield well in the autumn…" He stopped. "Forgive me. I want to show you everything, but of course I can't until you are well. Do you think you will be able to join us for dinner today in the great hall? Everyone meets there at midday, and so many people have asked about you. If they only saw that you are well, or on the way to it…"

If she could spend half the night making love with Zoticus, she could easily sit at a high table for an hour. She might need help getting there, but she could work that part out later. "Sure," she said.

"Wonderful!" Tobias kissed her cheek. "Thank you, Mother. Some of the children are so scared, they think you have the plague! Where they came up with such a silly idea, I can't imagine."

Given she'd suspected the same thing, the scared children weren't as silly as Tobias thought, but she didn't say so.

"We'll be safe here. I shall tell everyone so at dinner," she said instead.

Thirty-Six

Zoticus stayed away as long as he could, but eventually his feet found their way back to Sara's chamber. Perhaps he should have asked her permission to heal her again, but she'd looked so peaceful last night, sleeping in his arms, and he couldn't bear the thought that his selfish night with her might delay her recovery, so he'd fed more blood to the amulet than was really wise.

He'd been lightheaded when he made his way back up to his own cold bed, but it was for the best. Lady Sara was the virtuous widow everyone looked up to, and he would not take her reputation from her. She would have the strength to lead what remained of her people when it was time to return to her town, and he would be gone.

But instead of doing the sensible thing and creeping out the gate last night, he'd weakened himself so much from the blood loss that he'd decided to delay for another day.

The sight of her now was enough to make him both regret and rejoice in his decision.

She wore a fawn wool gown today, which looked golden in the sunlight streaming through the open window. Someone – heaven forbid she'd done it herself – had opened the shutters for her, and she sat in a chair before the window, where she might admire the view over the valley.

Then she saw him, and the smile that lit her face sent a bolt right through his heart. "Zoticus! I feared you were too busy to come see me today, and I need your help. I promised my son I would attend the midday meal in the great hall, but I suspect I will need your help getting there. Crossing the room and donning some clothes was not too taxing, but finding my way around an unfamiliar castle...I fear I might get lost and not have the strength to return to where someone might find me."

His heart sank. So his healing last night had not been enough to ward off any ill effects from their lovemaking. He'd have to heal her again today, before he departed.

"I'll take you down to the great hall, and bring you back when you are ready," he said.

He expected her to rise and walk with him, but she just sat in her seat, looking up at him expectantly.

She wanted him to take her in his arms again. Even after he'd exhausted her last night.

He swallowed. Then, selfish wretch that he was, he scooped her up and carried her out of the room.

She felt even softer clad in warm wool than she had last night. It took every bit of his willpower not to turn around and take her back to bed, where he would join her and...

No. If she didn't appear at dinner, someone would come looking, find them together, and that would not end well for her.

So he forced himself to march right down to the great hall, ascend the dais, and set her in the place of honour at the centre of the table. Tobias's usual place, until today.

Her fingers wrapped around his arm, tugging him down to her level. He expected her to say something for only his ears, but first she kissed his cheek before she said, "Thank you," loud enough for anyone nearby to hear.

He glanced around. Some of the children had entered the hall, finding their seats. Then someone caught sight of Sara, sitting at the high table, and the excited chatter began.

Zoticus wanted to sit at her side, as close as possible, ready to help her in an instant, should she need him, but he forced himself to move down the table, to the furthest seat to her left, where he might watch her without being so conspicuous.

The Younger Council, as he called them, to distinguish them from their predecessors in Mirroten, entered the hall. Tobias and Silvana sat on Sara's right and left hands, and the others took their places along the bench until there was no space left, except for the careful distance the brewer's boy kept between himself and Zoticus.

When everyone was seated, Tobias rose to his feet. "I want to thank everyone for all their work over the last week, preparing the castle for the coming winter and helping with the harvest. We may be here until the spring, or longer, depending on how long before the plague is gone and we may go home, but when we depart, we must make sure that the monastery is better supplied than when we arrived. And to guide us in our preparations, joining us today is my mother, Mistress Sara!"

Applause and cheers rang out across the hall.

Zoticus frowned. Sara was still recovering. She could not be expected to shoulder the burden of setting an entire castle in order is such a short time.

Raphael raised his cup. "A toast to Mistress Sara's health!" he shouted.

The whole hall followed suit, then drank deeply.

Sara smiled graciously through it all, but when they sat down, she scanned the crowd, searching for someone. Once, twice, three times her gaze circled the room, before she saw something that turned her face deathly pale.

Zoticus was on his feet, striding to her side before he could think. "Lady Sara is easily tired, and must return to her chamber to rest," he shouted. She did not resist as he lifted her from the chair and spirited her out of the room.

It wasn't until he laid her in her bed that he dared to breathe again. "What's wrong?" he demanded.

Her voice came out half strangled. "It's Tola, and her daughter, Swanhild. I didn't see them in the hall. Did they not make it to the monastery?" Tears spilled from her eyes.

Zoticus racked his brain, but he could not remember seeing them at all. "Swanhild wasn't among the children in the church. I don't think either of them joined our pilgrimage."

Sara started to sob. He hesitated only a moment before he pulled her into his arms to let her cry into his chest.

"Tola and Swanhild are witches. They have

powers normal people do not. If anyone can survive a plague, it's a witch. They are likely in hiding somewhere, too, waiting for it to be safe to go home. If you wish, I will go and search for them, and wherever they are hiding, I will find them, and send them home to you," he said. It was the least he could do for her when he left – send her friend back to her.

She sat up, sniffling. "What would I do without you, Zoticus?"

She'd do everything she did before she met him, he suspected, and her life would go back to normal. It was for the best.

Thirty-Seven

Zoticus soon left, saying something about getting her some food. Sara expected him to return, but Sal brought up her tray instead, asking after her health and telling her how much more complicated it was running a castle kitchen compared to helping her mother in the inn back home.

Several hours later, Sal returned, swapping the empty dinner tray for Sara's supper, but Zoticus was still absent.

"Do you know where Zoticus is?" Sara asked her.

Sal shrugged. "Master Zoticus is most mysterious, but in the mornings, he comes down a flight of stairs near the kitchen. I suspect his bedchamber is at the top of those stairs."

Sara thanked the girl, trying not to show her disappointment. She knew those stairs led to her own bedchamber, not Zoticus's.

But it couldn't hurt to take a look.

She closed the door, so no one would see, before pulling the tapestry aside. A spiral stair wound its way past the exposed archway, heading both up and down.

Down to the kitchens…up to where?

She craned her neck and thought she might see some light at the top, but she wasn't sure.

Was she well enough to ascend the stairs, to see what lay at the top? She could always stop and rest on the way, if she needed to.

One turn, then another, and partway around a third before she emerged into a round room, barely big enough for the pallet that took up most of the floor. Zoticus's sack of belongings sat beside it, and his cloak hung from a peg on the wall. The shuttered windows were all closed, but the light she'd seen came from a candle left burning beside his bed.

It looked like his room at the inn, or the cellar at the mill where he'd been held prisoner. Like he'd just left a moment ago, and he didn't intend to come back.

He'd talked of going to search for Tola and Swanhild. Surely he hadn't…

Sara fell to her knees on the pallet. "Please, no," she whimpered.

"What are you doing here?"

His footsteps were so silent, she hadn't known he was on the stairs until he spoke.

Something told her she should stand up, but Sara stubbornly stayed on her knees. "I came looking for you. You're leaving, aren't you?"

He inclined his head. "Of course. My work here is done. You and the children of your town are safe, the plague ships are burned, and the Bishop of Rialto wants a word with me. I thought I'd head down to Rialto, and tell him the only word I have for him is no, and maybe find your friend. Then, who knows? There are plenty of wicked knights in the world who are still breathing. I'd like to see how many I can stop."

"Did last night mean nothing to you? You said you loved me. Was that a lie?" she challenged him.

His shoulders slumped, and her heart sank along with them. She'd been a fool to believe him.

"Last night was wondrous, and I shall remember it all my days. Whether I love your or not, it does not matter, for an infamous assassin and a virtuous widow have no future together."

"Did you lie to me?" She had to know.

"Lady Sara, I have never lied to you. I love you as I have never loved any other woman, and I will treasure the one night fate allowed us to share together. Which is why I must leave you here where you will be safe, while I go and do…all the things an assassin does. Things of which you do not approve."

"If you leave, I would go with you."

"You cannot. They need you here."

She snorted. "They do not. Tobias has already taken leadership of the young people of Mirroten, and there are others who have already formed his council. You saw that as well as I did today. They will not be children much longer, and when they realise that, they will not need me."

He froze, his eyes fixed on the wall or on something far away. A vision, Sara realised.

"What did you see?" she demanded.

He dropped to his knees on the pallet, too. "The same as I always see. If I leave, you will run across the bailey in your black travelling cloak. Whether I will it or no, you will follow me." He closed his eyes. "Sara, I must keep you safe. You must stay here."

She grasped his hands in hers. "Only if you stay here with me."

He met her gaze. "I'm a selfish man, Sara. If I stay, it is only a matter of time before I am tempted to share your bed again. What will the children…what will your son say when he finds out?"

"Does it matter? I've spent my whole life caring for their town. You saved them. Don't you think we're owed a little happiness? And if we find it together, who has the right to judge us?"

Zoticus still didn't smile. "Well, the Bishop of Rialto, for one. If he is not happy with me, he might come after you."

"The Bishop of Rialto relies on my generosity to keep this monastery going. If he comes after me, he will soon find it very injurious to his purse. Not to mention, if he'd sent word earlier about Altino, he might have saved the people of our town. He will not like me laying those deaths at his door. He's always coveted my family's lands. Perhaps he delayed so that Tobias and I would die along with the rest of Mirroten, and he might have my lands for himself. Well, he shall not have them. All he will have is the sharp edge of my tongue."

He stared at her in wonder. "Is there anything you do not have an answer for? Anything you actually fear?"

"Losing those I love."

"Could you love an assassin?"

She cocked her head. "Only if you come back downstairs to my bed. This pallet is a bit small for the two of us…"

"If I share your bed again, I will never want to leave."

She smiled. "Then we have a deal."

Zoticus shook his head. "You drive a hard bargain, Lady Sara."

Sara laughed and reached under his tunic. "No, I believe the hardness is all yours."

Thirty-Eight

Just when Sara seemed to finally have recovered, she fell ill again. Instead of coughing, infection or the plague, however, this illness made her unable to eat without being terribly sick. She refused to drink anything but water, and no matter how much he used the healing amulet, it only seemed to make her worse.

"The sounds of me retching must have driven Tobias away from my door," Sara said one morning, when they emerged from her chamber to go down to breakfast.

Worry still ate at him, but that managed to make him laugh. "Oh, it's not you who drove him away, but a girl his own age who has caught his eye. He's been sleeping with the others, hoping to get closer to her, since the night we first made love, or he'd likely have broken down the door at the sound of your screaming."

Sara blushed. She had the saltiest tongue when they were alone in their bedchamber, but she still blushed like a maiden. "You surprised me, that's all. I did not expect you to be such an accomplished lover."

Zoticus snorted. "The first time, maybe. But by the seventh time, and every night after the first, you were definitely not surprised."

The smell of cooking wafted up the stairs.

Sara froze, then bolted back to her chamber. Zoticus found her noisily throwing up in the chamber pot.

He dug out a rag for her to wipe her mouth and handed it to her when she was finished.

Sara stared at the rag for a moment. "How long since I've had my monthly courses?"

Zoticus shrugged. "You haven't had them

since we arrived. I didn't realise you still had those. When women reach a certain age, they usually stop, leaving more nights for lovemaking." He wasn't going to complain. For three months he'd shared Sara's bed, and he knew he never wanted to leave it.

She swatted him lightly. "Yes, but I'm not that old. I still get them, or I did…you said once that the amulet let you sense the blood coursing through my veins, when I had that infection. Could you…could you use it to see if there is something else growing inside me?"

She climbed up on the bed, tugging the skirt of her gown up over her waist, baring her belly and everything beneath.

Zoticus's breath caught in his throat. He wanted to take his own clothes off and…

"The amulet," she reminded him.

Right. In a moment, then.

He pulled out the amulet, and she guided his hand down to her belly. For someone who ate so little, it made no sense for it to be rounded. Not as soft as he remembered, either. A chill went down his spine. There were other incurable diseases, worse than the plague, that he also could not heal. No, not Sara…

He could hear his heart racing, the opposite of her slow, steady beat. No, a heart rate that fast would have him breathing hard and feeling like it was bursting out of his chest.

He placed his spare hand at his throat, feeling for the rapid flutter he knew he should find there.

But his pulse kept pace with Sara's.

"I'm pregnant, aren't I?" Sara asked.

Pregnant? How?

Now he knew what to look for, he moved the amulet lower, and there she was. Heart beating like a frightened bird, tiny arms and legs reaching out for a hug she could not yet have, and all of her seemed to twinkle, like she was made up of a million tiny stars, sitting just beneath her skin…

Absolutely magical.

"She's beautiful," Zoticus breathed. His daughter. His and Sara's daughter. Which meant all those magic sparkles… "She's an enchantress. So much magic in her blood, she cancels out anything I can do with the amulet." Memory twinged, the shared magical memories from so many generations. "While you carry her, your blood mingles with hers. You should wear the amulet. It will heal you both, more than I ever could." He hung it around her neck, then helped her smooth down her skirts. "Let's go down to breakfast. If you're eating for two, you cannot miss a meal."

Sara shook her head, a look of wonder on her face. "I never thought I'd have another child. Not after Tobias. And a girl, too…she'll be born in the spring. If Tola were here, she'd be my midwife, or even Swanhild, but without them…I think I'm the only one here who has handled a birth before. And I'll be in too much pain to do everything myself. Where will we find a midwife?"

The first snowfall had closed the road the week before – not even the monks would be getting through until spring.

"I will do it. I've helped on a few deliveries before. My mother was the village healer, and she did most of them, but women would go into labour at the same time, and I knew enough to handle the easy ones…" Zoticus heard himself say the words, but they did not console him. This was Sara, not some peasant woman popping out her twentieth child from hips so wide she took up two places on a bench. "I'll find you a midwife, even if I have to dig through snow from here to Rialto. You and our daughter will be fine, I promise." The words felt right, though worry still niggled at him.

Sara's lips touched his, and all other thoughts flew away. "Thank you," she said. "You keep delivering miracles. Saving us, saving me, and now…you've given me the sweetest gift of all. A daughter I'd never dared hope for. If there were a priest in the castle, I'd make him marry us right now, for everything I have, everything I am…I would give you, and it would not be enough, to repay you for such a gift."

His heart soared. Yes, if he could marry any woman, he'd want Sara, but she'd never be safe. All it would take was one unscrupulous would-be client who threatened her life, and Zoticus would be forced to assassinate someone he did not want to kill. Worse, they might hurt Sara…

He would not let that happen.

But now was not the time or place, and there was no priest present, so he forced a smile upon his face as he said lightly, "Wait until the mite is born before you thank me. I'm told babies do nothing but cry and steal your sleep, not to mention the ordeal of her birth. You'll be cursing me, come spring, I'm certain of it."

Sara's smile only grew wider. "Come spring, she'll steal your heart as surely as you hold mine. You'll see."

He would, but he hoped he'd find a midwife well before then. He might have healed Sara once, but he knew he'd be tempting fate to take her health in his hands again.

Thirty-Nine

As Zoticus dug his way through the snow covering the road for what felt like the hundredth time that year, he cursed. He hated snow, he hated ice, and more than anything else, he hated the sulphur-coloured clouds heading their way that would likely dump another load of the stuff, undoing all his good work. Wasn't it supposed to be spring already?

If the snow didn't thaw soon, he knew he'd be delivering Sara's baby. He'd tried to confine her to her chamber, or even just the castle, but she was having none of it. Three times a day, she waddled out to the duckpond, determined to have eggs if the ducks had laid any. He lived in constant dread that she'd slip on the ice, or the stairs, or trip over one of the baby goats that no one seemed able to control. He'd even gone through his magic pouch, trying to find something that would keep her safe, or at least help her keep her balance. All he'd found was a cloak pin enchanted to keep the rain off whoever wore it, and Sara wasn't silly enough to go out in the rain.

She was, however, perfectly happy to waddle out for the second time today, wearing his warmest grey cloak, for it was the only one wide enough to fasten over her enormous round belly. Her words, not his, but no matter how much he agreed with her, he wasn't brave enough to say so where she might hear.

She disappeared around the corner of the woodshed, and Zoticus went back to work, shovelling snow.

A flash of light in the corner of his eye made him turn. If there'd been anything but clear skies there, he'd have thought he'd seen lightning, but he couldn't have. The storm clouds were still on the other side of the valley.

A shriek reached his ears – that sounded like Sara. He dropped his shovel and ran toward the woodshed.

Another flash of light, on the far side of the woodshed, followed by silence.

He rounded the corner, to find no one there. Sara's footprints just ended, as though a giant eagle had swooped in and carried her off.

Oh God, she hadn't fallen into the duckpond…

No, it was still frozen over, and yards away.

"Sara!" he shouted. "Sara!"

Zoticus staggered through the snow, searching for some sign of where she'd gone. He found Raphael near the kitchen gardens, shovelling snow away from the plants. "Have you seen Sara?" he asked.

Raphael leaned on his shovel, thoughtful. "I don't think I've seen her today, but she did ask for some willow bark to be sent up, and water to make tea. But that was hours ago. I imagine if she has a headache, though, she'd have stayed in her chamber. Have you checked there?"

Zoticus wasn't sure whether to laugh or cry in frustration. The only times Sara stayed in her chamber were when she was asleep or making love with him. She wouldn't be there now. Not when he'd just seen her in the courtyard.

One of the younger girls – Zoticus guessed she might be six or seven – raced through the kitchen door, skidded across the ice patch outside, then broke into a run on the snow without breaking stride.

"Master Zoticus, Master Zoticus!" she shouted.

"I'm here, child. What is it? Is it Lady Sara?"

He hoped so, but she'd come from inside the castle. It couldn't be.

"Mistress Dalia demands your presence in the best bedchamber right now!"

Mother. No, it couldn't be.

"Who did you say wants me?" he asked carefully.

The panic in the girl's voice grew. "Mistress Dalia, the midwife, says you must attend her right now!"

He wasn't a praying man, but if there was

one midwife he'd wanted here, it would be her. What she couldn't cure with her normal skills, she might with magic.

"Thank you," he said, breaking into a run. He jumped the ice patch, skidding a little on the step, before taking the stairs two at a time to the upper levels. He could scarcely breathe by the time he reached the door to Sara's chamber, but…

"Heavens, it hurts!"

That was Sara's voice, raw with pain.

"Well, if that boy would hurry up and get here, he might be able to do something about that!"

He had to smile. His mother was the only person in the world who'd call him a boy.

"Finally!" Mother snapped when he walked in. "Get over here and help your wife up. She's about to have your baby, so the least you can do is hold her in the right position so it hurts less!"

He considered correcting her, but the pained groan that came out of Sara made him forget everything else. Whether she was his wife or not, he'd help her get through this however he had to. Thank the Heavens his mother was here to help.

He drew Sara off the bed, careful to support her weight as she stood up, before she doubled over in pain as another contraction gripped her. This was where most husbands panicked, needing to be sent out of the room in search of something that took a long time to find, sometimes quite forcefully. Zoticus understood some of their panic – he wished he didn't have to see Sara in so much pain – but he'd be damned before anyone sent him away. It might take all his strength to bear her weight when she wanted to collapse with each contraction, but he'd hold her, for as long as it took.

"After this, I don't want any more children," Sara said, before the next contraction caught her in its toils.

"Never fear, she'll be your last," Mother said, dropping to her knees at Sara's feet. She'd laid a pile of cloths on the cold stone, ready to catch the baby. There were more draped over a bench beside the fire, warming in readiness to swaddle the child when she was born. "Now,

Sara, it's time to push."

The sounds that came from Sara's throat were more animal than human as she strained and pushed until finally, when his arms felt like they'd fall off after holding her up so long, a shrill child's scream rose from the floor.

With her red, scrunched-up face and bloody fluid coating her body, the girl looked more like a demon than a human, but Zoticus didn't care. He knew she'd be the most beautiful girl in his world before the day was done.

"Take care of the baby, Tick, while I deal with the afterbirth," Mother ordered.

He didn't hesitate. He scooped up the angry, bawling baby, and wrapped her in the softest, warmest cloth on the bench. When she seemed likely to wriggle free, he added a second cloth, but it just wouldn't wrap right. It had been so long since he'd helped with a birth, and he'd never been given the baby before. There must be some trick to it, something his mother hadn't taught him, but it was buried in his magical memories somewhere, if only he could find it.

"Give her to me." Sara's voice was soft and

hoarse, but he did not dare disobey her order.

He turned, to find Sara sitting up in bed, her arms out in readiness.

Wordlessly, he handed the child to her mother.

It took scarcely a moment for Sara to wrap the baby properly, before putting the child to her breast.

Zoticus's breath caught in his throat. He'd never seen a more beautiful sight. The woman he loved holding their child.

"Stop staring at her breasts, Tick, and go get your wife some dinner. She's just fought the battle of her life, and she's eating for two. See that the meat is well-cooked, and that there is not too much wine with it."

He wanted to stay, but he knew it wasn't worth his life to disobey. Not with both women ordering him about.

When he reached the bottom of the stairs, he met Tobias and Silvana. "Is Sara all right?" Silvana asked. "Raphael said she'd gone into labour."

Zoticus broke into a smile. "Sara is well, and so is the baby. A girl. She's resting now, but they are both well." And in the best possible hands, he added to himself. He skipped the rest of the way to the kitchen, determined to bring Sara the best, heartiest meal he could provide.

Forty

Sara waited until Zoticus was out of earshot before she said, "You're mistaken. I'm not his wife."

Dalia waved a hand like she was shooing away a fly. "Pah, but you will be. My Tick has done some foolish things in his life – that cold bitch Gemma, for one – but finding you is not one of them. He's still an assassin, with all the dangers that come with that job, but he'll always come back to you. He loves you."

Sara's breath caught in her throat. "You mean I'll lose him, just like my first husband."

She didn't think her heart could bear losing him, too.

Dalia chuckled. "Oh, no, you'll never lose him. True to his name, my Tick will stick to you until the end of your days. He'll outlive us all, you'll see. You, me, even his twin sister, Zoraida. This little one and Zoraida's daughters will be the only ones left when he's an old, old man, dying in his sleep."

Sara allowed herself to breathe again. "I'd ask how you know, but he has the gift of future sight. I take it he inherited it from you?"

Dalia nodded. "Tick always kept his gifts secret. No one outside the family knew he had magic at all. If he's told you, he already considers you family. He'll make you his wife, soon enough."

Sara wasn't so sure, but she didn't think it wise to argue with Zoticus's mother. Not only had she just delivered her baby, but she was a powerful enchantress who could probably turn her into a newt if she offended her. "Why do you call him Tick?" she asked instead.

"Twas Zoraida's doing. She complained that he always followed her and her friends around like a bothersome tick, when they were small children, and somehow the name stuck. Of course, it's no sort of name for a fearsome assassin, and it did not make him popular with the girls in the town where he grew up, but my Zoticus has made his name known and feared all about the world. I think more people fear him than his sister, though she has magic and he has little of it. Funny how things turn out." She fixed Sara with her steely eye. "Now, speaking of names, what do you intend to name my granddaughter?"

"I'd thought Rossa, after my mother, who had red hair, but I wanted to discuss it with Zoticus first…"

Dalia nodded. "Rossa. I like it. As will he, when he's done getting you the fanciest dinner the castle kitchens can provide. But I sent him away so that I might have a word."

Sara pressed her lips together and nodded. Her mother in law might say many words, but Sara's word was law here, and once her mother in law left, Sara would decide what might happen, not Dalia.

"Now, little Rossa here is a witch. A mighty

powerful one, like her aunt and her cousin. Likely she'll be an enchantress, too, able to cast portals and any other spell she turns her hand to. She'll have a fairy godmother, most likely Zoraida's girl, Zuleika. I wish I could do it, but I won't live long enough to be there when she needs me. She'll have you and Zoticus, and that's good."

Sara found herself nodding. She'd have to ask Zoticus about enchantresses, and how to stop one from lighting the house on fire or shaking apart the mountain when she threw a tantrum. Cousins…she could deal with when she met them. She shifted so that she could switch the baby to her other breast, and hissed as pain erupted from her nether regions.

Dalia blinked. "By all that's holy, I forgot to heal you. Don't tell Tick!" She dipped her hand in the bucket that held the afterbirth, and it came up dripping with blood. She seized the healing amulet that hung around Sara's neck in her bloody hand, and held it tight for a long moment.

Sara felt a tingling sensation start in her chest, then spread like lightning through her body. Heat built uncomfortably in her nether regions, but it faded quickly, taking the pain with it, leaving Sara gasping.

"Little Rossa's blood is more powerful than Tick's," Dalia said knowingly.

It was like comparing a candle to the sun. When she was ill, he'd healed her over an entire week, and she'd still felt tired. Now…she feared if she could listen to her heart, she'd hear her blood singing in her veins.

"When she's old enough, give her the amulet to wear always. It will heal her, like it healed Zoticus, even if she's on the cusp of death." Dalia laid a box on the bed. "I brought you some wedding gifts, too. Seeing as I won't be invited to your wedding."

Sara lifted the lid. Inside sat a black wool cloak, lined with silk, and fastened with a silver pin in the shape of a flower. "They're very fine. Thank you."

Dalia make an impatient sound in her throat. "Yes, they're fine, such as might be worn by a lady of your station, but it's the magic in them that makes them valuable. The brooch will heal you, much like the amulet does my son or your daughter, but there is no blood price to pay. I already paid it when I laid the enchantment on it. The cloak itself will be your armour. I placed a powerful protection spell on the cloth, so that as long as you are wearing it, nothing can harm you. The spell is not confined to the cloth, but the one who wears it. So if you were to simply drape it over your shoulders, and a rock fell from the mountain onto your head, the rock would bounce off and would not touch you.

"You'll never need the brooch, though you may find it useful. The cloak will keep you safe from Tick's enemies, and those who wish to control him through you."

Dread seized Sara's heart. "What about Rossa? Or my son?"

"Rossa will grow into her powers quickly enough. She's using them already. Look." Dalia pointed at the window.

All manner of birds sat on the sill, jostling for position, yet all staring at Rossa. Songbirds, scavenger birds, someone's hunting hawk and an eagle that normally lived high up on the mountain. Even an owl joined the strange flock.

Sara shivered. There was magic at work here – powers she did not understand.

Dalia rose. "Well, that's all, I think. If I think of anything else, I'll portal back here, but Tick is surprisingly capable for a man. He'll help you more than you know, though you still might have to tell him what to do from time to time. Take care of that little girl."

She waved, then drew a circle with her hand. A sparkling portal appeared, just as it had by the duckpond when Sara had felt her first contraction. Dalia stepped through it, and disappeared.

"Thank you," Sara said. Too late for Dalia to hear her, but no less heartfelt.

Forty-One

Three years ago, if anyone had told him he'd spend more than a day in a monastery, Zoticus would have laughed at them. Yet he'd spent two years living here with Sara, and as summer faded into autumn once more, he wondered how much longer it would be before it was safe to venture down from the mountains to see who else had survived the plague.

They'd had no contact with anyone outside the monastery since they'd arrived, and more than once, he'd caught the others discussing whether there was anyone else left.

Most of them had moved out of the monastery, though, and last summer, a village had sprung up where a patch of forest had once stood. Some of the older children were children no more, forming their own households with their younger siblings…and a few had even taken a partner. With no priest to celebrate weddings, though, he wasn't sure how long the pairings would survive. Another summer? Or their entire lives?

He suspected Tobias and the miller's girl were one of the pairs likely to last. Likely because Silvana ruled the roost in their cottage.

Some, like himself and Sara, had stayed in the castle, but they'd moved from the monks' dormitories to more private accommodation when the weather was warmer.

Raphael had taken the solar atop the highest tower, and he was up there most days. Watching for what or whom, Zoticus did not know, but there was a yearning in the man's eyes that said he would not be settling into the new village any time soon.

He was up there now, hanging out the window, shouting and waving and pointing at the road.

Had someone finally come to the monastery?

Zoticus clambered to the top of the bailey wall, so that he might see the travellers. Sure enough, he could see a party approaching, with wagons, horses and many men on foot. Too far away to see who, though.

Instinct took over. He might not have taken any commissions lately, but he'd been an assassin for too long to forget years of training, or to want to wear any colour other than his customary grey. Today, it allowed him to disappear into the shadows, leaning against the parapet that gave a guard the best view over the gate.

He could always close the gate, for news could be shouted from outside the wall, but something told him to leave it open.

"What's happening? What do you see?" Sara called up.

So much for being well hidden. She saw him, no matter what.

"There's someone coming up the road. A large party, like we were when we arrived."

Sara frowned. "I'll go get my cloak."

Which meant she was worried, and wanted the protective enchantment his mother had laid on the cloak. He wasn't going to argue – he'd do anything to keep her safe.

Slowly, the travellers ambled closer. They evidently weren't in any hurry to reach the monastery's walls. Perhaps they weren't fleeing the plague, and it was safe to leave. Maybe even return to Mirroten.

"Master Zoticus? Can you see them? I think there's someone important coming. All brightly coloured on a big white horse!" Raphael climbed the bailey wall, then pointed.

Zoticus was loath to admit the young man's eyesight was far better than his. "Do you recognise him?"

Raphael smiled sadly. "Who would I know important enough to own a horse like that? He's surely some nobleman. Maybe a prince, or even the king!"

If it was the king, it was a good thing Zoticus hadn't closed the gates. Kings weren't particularly fond of being shut out of parts of their own kingdom. But a royal party would be larger, with more horses, for knights did not walk when they could ride.

Whoever they were, he hoped they'd brought a priest. Tobias and Silvana, as well as some of the other young couples, were eager to wed.

Zoticus shaded his eyes. If he wasn't mistaken, the man on the white horse wore the Bishop of Rialto's colours. He could not yet see the man's face, but he wouldn't have been surprised if it was the bishop himself. Most of the men with him wore the drab tunics that marked them as monks. So some of them had survived the plague, then…or these were new ones, come to claim the monastery as their own.

"Rossa! Get back here! Rossa!"

The girl had taken more than a year to learn to walk, but it had only taken her a day to learn to run. Rossa came barrelling out of the door to the great hall, giggling madly, with Sara a few steps behind.

"Daddy!" the girl shrieked, heading straight for Zoticus, heedless of the riders already entering the bailey.

"Rossa!" Sara screamed, sprinting down the steps. The wind whipped her cloak behind her, so it looked like wings.

His vision. Zoticus dropped down to the bailey and scooped up his wayward daughter, turning his back on the new arrivals to take Rossa back to her mother.

"Out of the way, peasant! His Excellency, the Bishop of Rialto, is here to take possession of his new lands. Show some respect!"

That was a mistake. Zoticus turned to grin at the idiot who'd spoken.

The Bishop of Rialto's horse, however, distracted them all by rearing up and dumping His Excellency on his ample arse in the dust.

There was magic in the air, and he had not used any. Zoticus shot a sideways glance at Sara, wondering if her cloak had done it, but found his daughter staring fixedly at the horse, who was now back on all four hooves, bowing his head in her direction.

Interesting.

Zoticus stepped forward and held out his hand to help the bishop up. "What are you doing here, Ambrose?"

The bishop reached out to take his hand, then paled and shrank back. "Master Zoticus? I'd heard that you died with the rest of Mirroten!"

Sara's soft gasp at this bald statement of bad news hardened his heart against the bishop. And what was this about the bishop's new lands? These lands belonged to Sara's family. Unless the bishop and the king believed she was dead...

Zoticus's grin grew wider. "Maybe the people who stayed in Mirroten died, but most of the town survived by coming up here to the stronghold. Including Lady Sara and her son, Tobias."

The bishop turned whiter than the snowcapped mountains behind the castle. "S-s-survived?"

"Oh yes." Zoticus held out his hand to Sara as he executed his best courtly bow. "Lady Sara, may I present Bishop Ambrose of Rialto? Ambrose, this is Lady Sara and her daughter, Lady Rossa."

He wasn't sure how well versed Sara was in political intrigue, but she understood well enough that when he'd introduced the bishop to her, instead of the other way around, he'd been telling her she outranked the man. She merely stood and stared, instead of curtseying, like the bishop evidently expected.

Muttering a curse under his breath, the bishop heaved himself to his feet, then managed a clumsy bow in her direction. "Lady Sara. It is a miracle indeed that the Lord chose to save you from the plague that killed so many."

She inclined her head just the slightest bit. The queen herself would have been proud. "Maybe a miracle, or maybe it is merely good planning. Master Zoticus brought word of the terrible tragedy that befell Altino, and helped by his good advice, we came here, where we've been safe. Sadly, not all the town chose to leave, and I am saddened to hear that those poor misguided souls have paid a terrible price for not listening to wise Master Zoticus."

Zoticus wanted to applaud, but he forced his hands to stay by his sides.

The bishop's face turned red. "My dear Lady Sara, you cannot possibly be serious! Zoticus is neither wise or good. The man is an assassin, and you are lucky he has not murdered you all in your beds! I insist on taking him back to Rialto with me, where he will face justice for his crimes. If you have placed your trust in such a vile criminal, it is only by a miracle indeed that you have survived!"

Zoticus opened his mouth to demand that the bishop answer such an insult with his sword. He'd never murdered anyone in their beds. His hand clenched on the hilt of his own blade, ready to draw it.

Sara's hand squeezed his, keeping the sword firmly in its sheath.

She laughed. "Oh, you are most entertaining, Bishop Ambrose! To think someone has made up such malicious stories about dear, kind Master Zoticus. Why, every person here owes Zoticus their life, some of us twice over. Had he committed any crime here, I would have seen to it that justice was served, for I am, of course, the landowner here. But justice is a sword with two edges, one for punishment, and one for reward. Thus, for his services to me and my people, I have resolved to give him my hand in marriage. It would be most fitting if you would celebrate the marriage rites for us, here in the castle my family built, that has sheltered us in our time of need. This very afternoon. I insist."

Yesterday, Zoticus might have protested about the danger he'd place Sara in by marrying her. Today, he felt the peculiar urge to kneel before her and pledge his sword to her protection. Lady Sara had finally come into her own, and he'd be honoured to be her husband.

The bishop looked from Sara to Zoticus, as if he wasn't sure who frightened him most. "Yes, Lady Sara. Of course. I would be honoured. Ah, but about the castle. You see, I brought some monks, thinking this place was still a monastery…"

"After the wedding, my dear bishop. It is not fitting to speak to a bride about business. In fact, it might be more fitting that you ask my husband…"

The bishop was likely to die of apoplexy before he left the monastery, Zoticus suspected, judging by how red the man's face grew. He couldn't find it in his heart to feel sorry for the man, either. He could have sent word of Altino's demise all along the river, so that all the towns would have known to turn travellers away. Instead, he'd let them all die, only telling Mirroten when it was too late to save them. If Zoticus had not arrived, Sara and all the others might have died…all in keeping with the vile bishop's plan.

"Oh, you must wait until at least after the honeymoon," Zoticus said, entering the game. "Such an honour, and such a noble bride, I will scarcely know what to do with myself, let alone my lady's lands. Perhaps we shall keep this castle for ourselves."

The bishop appeared to have difficulty drawing breath. Zoticus recognised the signs of impending death. He had only to continue in the same vein, and it would be assured.

By the time the bishop's attendants realised what was happening and Sara called for a healer, it was too late.

A good man might have felt guilt, but Zoticus had been an assassin for a long time, and he had no sympathy for men who played games with other people's lives.

"Is there a priest present? I think the poor bishop needs someone to administer his last rites," Zoticus said.

"And conduct the wedding, if the poor bishop cannot," Sara said.

A priest was produced, a young man who stammered his way through the Latin with all the quivering dread of a man who believed he'd be next if he didn't obey, and the bishop's soul was sent to his maker. Or the devil. Zoticus left such matters up to those who understood them.

Before the sun had set, his own soul had been wedded to Sara's, and several other couples had come forward to take their vows, so a wedding feast was laid out in the great hall, to be shared between monks and the survivors of Mirroten.

As Zoticus surveyed the hall from the high table, in the seat of honour with his wife by his side, he wished he'd been able to save more. But in the battle between one man and a plague…he felt it was fair to call this a victory.

About the Author

Demelza Carlton has always loved the ocean, but on her first snorkelling trip she found she was afraid of fish.

She has since swum with sea lions, sharks and sea cucumbers and stood on spray drenched cliffs over a seething sea as a seven-metre cyclonic swell surged in, shattering a shipwreck below.

Demelza now lives in Perth, Western Australia, the shark attack capital of the world.

The *Ocean's Gift* series was her first foray into fiction, followed by her suspense thriller *Nightmares* trilogy. She swears the *Mel Goes to Hell* series ambushed her on a crowded train and wouldn't leave her alone.

Want to know more? You can follow Demelza on Facebook, Twitter, YouTube or her website, Demelza Carlton's Place at:

www.demelzacarlton.com

Books by Demelza Carlton

Siren of Secrets series

Ocean's Secret (#1)

Ocean's Gift (#2)

Ocean's Infiltrator (#3

Siren of War series

Ocean's Justice (#1)

Ocean's Widow (#2)

Ocean's Bride (#3)

Ocean's Rise (#4)

Ocean's War (#5)

How To Catch Crabs

Nightmares Trilogy

Nightmares of Caitlin Lockyer (#1)

Necessary Evil of Nathan Miller (#2)

Afterlife of Alana Miller (#3)

Mel Goes to Hell series

The Devil's Work (#1)

See You in Hell (#2)

Mel Goes to Hell (#3)

To Hell and Back (#4)

The Holiday From Hell (#5)

All Hell Breaks Loose (#6)

The Devil Goes to Heaven (#7)

Romance Island Resort series
Maid for the Rock Star (#1)
The Rock Star's Email Order Bride (#2)
The Rock Star's Virginity (#3)
The Rock Star and the Billionaire (#4)
The Rock Star Wants A Wife (#5)
The Rock Star's Wedding (#6)
Maid for the South Pole (#7)

Romance a Medieval Fairytale series
Enchant: Beauty and the Beast Retold
Dance: Cinderella Retold
Fly: Goose Girl Retold
Revel: Twelve Dancing Princesses Retold
Silence: Little Mermaid Retold
Awaken: Sleeping Beauty Retold
Embellish: Brave Little Tailor Retold
Appease: Princess and the Pea Retold
Blow: Three Little Pigs Retold
Return: Hansel and Gretel Retold
Wish: Aladdin Retold
Melt: Snow Queen Retold
Spin: Rumpelstiltskin Retold
Kiss: Frog Prince Retold
Reflect: Snow White Retold
Roar: Goldilocks Retold
Cobble: Elves and the Shoemaker Retold
Float: Enchanted Horse Retold
Steal: Forty Thieves Retold
Call: Pied Piper Retold